Praise for Beth Williamson's *The Legacy*

5 Angels and Recommended Read   "...The Legacy, grabs you from the first page and doesn't let you go until the end. Beth Williamson pens a great western and puts you right beside her characters, living their lives and taking part in their adventures."

~ *Fallen Angels Reviews*

5 Blue Ribbons   "THE LEGACY is the seventh and final story in Beth Williamson's Malloy family series. I'm so sad to see this series end - it was this series that turned me onto Ms. Williamson's writing and I've never once been disappointed in any of her books. I've adored the entire Malloy family..."

~ *Romance Junkies*

5 Hearts   "Beth Williamson has fast become one of my absolute favorite authors; she is known for her historical westerns and this one is exceptional! ...This series has transported me back to the time of real cowboys; each book, as I read, was my favorite! I recommend you get the entire series, start with this one if you wish, and read them all! Noah and Rosalyn unquestionably upheld her high standards and I guarantee you will not be disappointed!"

~ *The Romance Studio*

4 Cups "The Legacy is a poignant story with so much depth and emotion that it is hard not to fall in love with Noah or Rosalyn ...Beth Williamson tells a lovely story filled with romance and passion that matures beautifully. She pens a tale that captivates and makes the reader feel as if they have stepped inside the adventure."

~ *Coffee Time Romance*

"Bummed to see the series end, proud to have read every book, I have to give big love to Beth Williamson for a truly wonderful end book. The Legacy was the perfect story for Noah. I am so glad he finally found the one place where he felt he belonged – Rosalyn's arms."

~ *Joyfully Reviewed*

The Legacy

Beth Williamson

A SAMHAIN PUBLISHING, LTD. publication.

Samhain Publishing, Ltd.
577 Mulberry Street, Suite 1520
Macon, GA 31201
www.samhainpublishing.com

The Legacy
Copyright © 2007 by Beth Williamson
Print ISBN: 1-59998-767-8
Digital ISBN: 1-59998-516-0

Editing by Sasha Knight
Cover by Scott Carpenter

First Samhain Publishing, Ltd. electronic publication: June 2007
First Samhain Publishing, Ltd. print publication: April 2008

Dedication

To my wonderful peeps for all their support, friendship and encouragement. Thank you Don, Janette, Allie, Nancy and Kristen! You all rock!

Prologue

September 1889, Wyoming

"Move!"

Noah Calhoun started in the saddle at the sound of his father shouting. The creak of leather ricocheted in the stillness around him.

"Noah, goddammit, *move now!"* Tyler rode toward him like a streak of black lightning. The sky behind his father whirled with shades of gray mixed with bruising purple as a storm approached. The air was full of electric energy, making the hairs on the back of his neck stand up.

Then Noah noticed the bull. Hercules was a mean son of a bitch that had forced more than a few cowboys to go see Doctor Brighton. This time the animal headed toward him, head down, death winking from the tips of its horns.

Noah froze, both terrified and mesmerized by the sight of two thousand pounds of pure bovine power tearing across the ground. Ripples of movement flowed through the muscles on the giant animal. Noah heard the sound of its breathing, imagined he could even feel the heat from its glistening hide.

"Noah!"

By the time Noah heard his father call him for the third time, Hercules was only six feet from him. Noah knew it was too late to escape completely, but he spurred his horse, Ringer, with everything he had.

The world slowed down and Noah realized two things. He'd never really been in love and he hadn't latched Hercules' gate. Two regrets he'd never be able to fix. Then the bull reached him and the horse screamed, throwing Noah off his back as the bull gored the poor thing. When the horse went down, Noah picked himself up with nary a breath left in his body and started running.

He didn't know how long he had, but he'd be damned if he didn't go down without at least making a run for it. The sound of the hooves echoed in his ears while the rumble of the earth beneath his feet made his skin pebble. He finally got his breath back and it exploded out of him on a sob. As the bull closed in, he darted right and then something slammed into him from the left.

As the breath whooshed from his body again, he grunted and rolled around on the ground, waiting for the pain from the horns. Instead, another horse screamed and his father shouted. Noah heard more hoofbeats and the whistles from other cowboys.

Ben, the oldest of his father's ranch hands, leaned over him. "Noah, you okay?"

Noah sucked in a shaky breath, surprised to find himself alive. "A little banged up, but I'm okay."

"Good, then you can help me with your father."

"Pa?" Noah scrambled to his feet, ignoring the body of his father's gelding that twitched and whickered.

His father lay with his life's blood coating the ground as Elmer, another ranch hand, stood over him. The sight was like a punch to the stomach. Pain roared through Noah and he dropped to his knees.

"Pa?" Noah whispered. He glanced up at a sad-eyed Elmer.

"It don't look good, boy."

Noah tore off his shirt, buttons flying every which way, and pressed the cloth to the gaping wound in Tyler's chest. Tears blurred his vision as he prayed to God his own stupidity hadn't killed his father.

Chapter One

May 1892, Chancetown, Wyoming

Noah Calhoun sipped the whiskey slowly, savoring the burn as it slid down his dry throat. Although it wasn't quite noon, he'd needed a drink and a little company. He glanced around—it was a typical watering hole with the same people in it he'd come to expect in every other saloon.

Another nameless, faceless town. So far, the lady bartender had been polite, but not friendly. Noah was down to the lint in his pocket and the eight bits that would buy him two more shots of whiskey.

He needed a job in the worst way.

"Hey, could I get another?" He held up the half-empty glass and smiled at the bartender.

She nodded and held up one finger. Noah was pleased she hadn't ignored him. He might have had to charm her, or at least try to. Uncle Trevor had taught him well.

Noah bided his time watching the other folks in the saloon. It was the usual mixture of cowpokes, working girls, locals and a few dark-looking fellas who generally caused trouble. It was the two in the dark corner, whispering and yanking the girls on their laps every five minutes, who worried him. No good could come of it, and his instincts were never wrong. It had saved his life more than once.

"That'll be four bits."

Noah hadn't even heard the bartender approach, and her voice surprised him. She was tall and thin with dark hair and eyes, and lines from a hard life etched in her face. Noah put her age at around forty, but for all he knew she could be twenty with too many hardships to count. With an apologetic grin, he fished into his pocket for the coins and put them on the bar. When she reached for them, he covered her hand with his.

"You know any ranches around here looking for help?"

She looked down at his hand and back at his face. One eyebrow rose. "You want to take your hand off me? I don't work on my back."

"I'm sorry, ma'am." He snatched his hand back. "My family was...is the kind that is affectionate, always touching and hugging. I forget other folks don't... Ah, forget all that. I sound plumb loco."

A small grin tugged the corner of her mouth. "It's past spring round-up, but I could ask around if you'd like."

Noah's smile was genuine. "That'd be right nice of you. I surely do appreciate that." He held out his hand. "Name's Noah Calhoun."

She shook it with a strong, calloused grip. "Marina Fuerte."

"Pleased to meet you, Marina. You work here long?"

"I own the place." She glanced around with pride. "Even if it is a lousy saloon."

"Oh, believe me, it's not lousy. I've been in places that are worse than an outhouse." Noah ran his hands along the polished, scarred bar. "This place is a palace and it's very clean."

"Thank you, Noah." Her eyes twinkled. "I appreciate the compliment."

With a nod, she went back to the other customers, leaving Noah to his thoughts. It had been almost three years since he'd left home and not a day went by that he didn't miss his family. His mother had understood why he couldn't stay, what drove him to set off on his own. The memory of his father nearly bleeding to death slammed into him and Noah closed his eyes, willing the image away.

"I said leave them alone. You get your ugly asses out of here." Marina's angry voice cut through Noah's self-imposed suffering.

"What if'n we don't want to?" The oily voice of one of the dark strangers skittered down Noah's spine.

He stood, straightening the Colts that rode his hips, and moved next to the rifle-toting bartender.

"You heard the lady. Git."

The two of them snickered. "I don't see no lady. Why don't you get lost, boy?"

"First of all, I'm not a boy. Second, I'm not going anywhere. You are." He widened his stance, hands hovering over the guns as he focused on what he needed to do. "I'll give you to the count of three."

Noah heard whispers of "Calhoun" and "bounty hunter". Obviously his father's reputation was still widely known. The two troublemakers looked at each other, then at him.

"One."

"Your pa really that bounty hunter?" One of them stepped closer to the door.

"Yes. Two."

"Maybe we ought to come back later when the gals are more friendly." The one closest to the door bolted before his friend could respond.

The second one stepped toward Noah, and in a flash the Colt was nestled in Noah's hand, cocked and aimed at the other man's head.

"I don't want any trouble, mister, and neither does Marina. Just go about your business someplace else." Noah kept his voice even and frosty.

The stranger's face hardened, full of malevolence and hate. "You ain't done with me yet, pup. Watch your back." He tossed chairs and people aside as he left the saloon, his hollow threats echoing around the room.

Noah watched the stranger's progress until the door swung behind him, then he let out a breath and lowered his gun. Thank God. He'd never had occasion to actually use the gun on a man before and hoped it wouldn't happen today.

"Thanks, Noah."

He turned toward Marina and shook his head. "I don't take kindly to folks like that. I had a feeling they weren't going to behave."

"Me either. I was keeping an eye on them." She inclined her head toward the bar. "I think I may have a job for you."

ಬ

Noah stared at the gray-haired man across from him. "I don't think I heard you right. What did you just say?"

The older man laughed. "I said you interested in the sheriff's job? I cain't work no more with my bad ticker and the town left it up to me to find somebody to take on the job. Marina here tells me you got what it takes. That's good enough for me. It pays fifty dollars a month."

Noah resisted the urge to slap himself to make sure he was awake. He couldn't possibly have understood the offer.

"Sheriff Boyton, you're telling me you'd hire a drifter off the street to protect your town?" Noah couldn't quite accept it. "I've never done any lawman work before."

"Eh, there ain't nothing to it. You can handle a gun, you're certainly big enough, and Marina likes you. And, ah, I actually know your father." The blue eyes twinkled a bit beneath the bushy brows. "Had occasion to deal with him once or twice."

Tyler Calhoun had been the best bounty hunter in Texas once upon a time. After he met and married his wife, Nicky, he hung up his guns. Even as Noah's adopted father, Tyler's name still carried weight years after retiring.

However, the questions whirling around Noah's brain had nothing to do with his father and everything to do with his own abilities. Yes, he could handle a gun, and he knew a thing or two about cowboys and their rough ways, but a lawman?

"I, um, are you sure you want me?" He glanced at Marina, who stood at the bar watching them. She winked and he had to control the urge to blush.

"I say we give it a try for a week or two and see what happens."

Noah had contemplated the dark road that held his future many nights. Most times he gave up, tired of trying to imagine what would come. This opportunity to be a sheriff hadn't ever been in those imaginings. Not for a moment.

He thought about his family and what they would say about it, which uncle would tease him, which young cousin would love to touch a shiny silver star. Most of all, he thought about what he might be able to do as a lawman, like help folks who were in trouble. Noah could have used a lawman like that when he was growing up. That thought was the one that made up his mind.

Noah held out his hand. "I'll take it."

"Hot damn." Sheriff Boyton shook his hand with a grip that belonged to a twelve-year-old girl, not a sixty-year-old man. He wasn't kidding when he said he needed to quit.

"You made a good choice, Johnny." Marina smiled at the sheriff's enthusiasm. "Congratulations, Noah."

"Thanks." Noah took his hand back and stared at the sheriff's badge in his hand.

Sheriff Noah Calhoun was on the job.

ℰↄ

The jail wasn't exactly what Noah had expected. The two cells likely hadn't been cleaned in a dog's age and the smell made Noah's nose wrinkle. He'd been in jail a time or two over the last three years, some worse than this one, but not many. The one in Kansas City at least had good food, although he'd only enjoyed it one night after being arrested for being too drunk. The jail in Westover, Colorado, came a close second to Chancetown. That particular place Noah had endured for a solid week while he waited for the circuit judge to arrive. The bar fight had been a particularly nasty one. He'd needed the time to heal and had to do it in a flea-infested cell.

Chancetown's jail put those two to shame in its filthiness. In fact, it was a pigsty.

The sheriff may have been good at his job, but he was a lousy housekeeper. His desk overflowed with wanted posters, papers, some crusty tin plates and several cups holding undetermined contents. After clearing his throat and giving

Noah a sheepish glance, the sheriff showed him around the building.

"This here's my desk and the papers and such that come in. I try to keep up with them, but lately there's been so many." He shook his silvery head. "Too many ne'er–do-wells thinking they can make their living with a gun."

The old sheriff walked over to the two cells and poked his head inside. "Hmm, could use a good cleaning." Noah resisted the urge to snort at the understatement. "Maybe you could ask Marina if one of her girls might be interested. There's a small apartment upstairs for ya. You can move your things in there."

Noah didn't mention that his things fit inside two saddlebags. He hadn't taken much with him when he left home, just a horse and some basics. His mother only asked that he send word now and then to make sure he was alive. Everything else he carried in his heart.

"You also get meals with the job. Just go to Elsa's restaurant down the street. I'll let her know who you are." The sheriff looked around, then back at Noah. "Any questions?"

Noah marveled at the good fortune that had fallen in his lap. A job, a place to sleep with a roof and free meals. What else could he ask for?

"I'll just mosey on along, then. I moved into the boardinghouse down the street a couple years ago. Couldn't get up those stairs no more. I'll be there for a day or two until you get settled, then I got me a little place just outside town that's waiting on me. You just come on down and see me if'n you need any help." After a brief handshake, the sheriff left Noah alone.

The sounds from the street were muffled, only an echo of wagons, horses and murmurs of conversation. Noah considered pinching himself, but decided that would be foolish. Dreams might not come true, but a fella had to wonder if God had something in mind sometimes.

He looked at the silver star in his hand, then rubbed it on his shirt to make it shine. The metal was a little worn, but it still gleamed, the word SHERIFF in fine letters. He swallowed the lump in his throat as he pinned it on his shirt.

Noah hoped his father would be proud of him. Even if the opportunity had fallen in his lap, Noah knew a gift when he received it. He spent the next couple of hours straightening up as best he could. It was still a mess and he apparently had no skill at cleaning up enormous clutter.

"Noah?"

He turned to find Marina and two other women at the door. Two working gals by the look of it, with flouncy, peek-a-boo clothes that left little to the imagination. One was blonde, the other a redhead in a color nature never intended.

"Howdy, ladies." Noah tipped his hat.

The two women tittered and poked each other in the arm.

"Oh, he's such a gentleman," the blonde one gushed.

"And so handsome too." The redhead put her finger between her teeth and gazed at him from under her lashes.

Noah backed up a step, ready to run for the hills if they attacked.

"Leave him alone, girls," Marina admonished. "Can't you see you're scaring him?" She smiled at Noah. "I wanted to come by and offer Bitsy and Cherry's services to you."

"Ah, services? Ladies, I appreciate the offer but as sheriff I don't think I can—"

Marina laughed, a sound that reminded him so much of his mother that his stomach clenched in pain. He didn't know why he was thinking of his parents so much but it had to stop.

"Not *that* kind of service." She winked. "They came to clean the place. I love Johnny Boyton, but the man lived like a pig in a wallow. For a dollar apiece, they'll have this place shining like a new penny in a couple of hours."

Noah licked his lips. "I, ah, don't have that much money, Marina. I'm not rightly sure when I'll get my pay."

"I understand." She glanced at the girls. "You two okay with waiting to get paid by Sheriff Calhoun?"

The blonde held out her hand. "I'm Bitsy, Sheriff, and I'd be happy to oblige you. I mean"—she giggled—"wait until you can *pay* me."

Cherry pushed her aside, one titian curl bouncing dangerously close to her eye. "I'll do it for free." She grinned as her gaze traveled up and down his body. "Oh yeah, I ain't charging you a dime."

Marina rolled her eyes. "Keep your hands to yourself, Cherry. You two get started in here. We've got hours until the saloon gets busy. I'm sure there's some soap and a scrub brush in here somewhere. If not, go down to the saloon and borrow some." She hooked her arm through Noah's. Her scent of soap and something sweet made him homesick again. "We're going to eat."

The two girls looked as if they wanted to argue, but they nodded and started whispering to each other while shooting glances at Noah. He let Marina march him out of the sheriff's office before a chuckle escaped.

"They're good girls. Really." She smiled. "You just have to know how to handle them."

"I'll take your word for it. I'm no good at handling women, period. You can ask any woman in my family." The laughter died on his lips when he realized what he'd said.

Marina stepped off the wood-planked sidewalk and headed across the road to the restaurant he'd seen when riding into town. A clean-looking place with lacey curtains in the window that lent it a homey feel. Her dark hair swayed softly on her shoulders as they walked.

"Where is your family?"

"Down state aways," he answered, purposely vague.

"You leave home for a reason or just to get off on your own?" She stopped just outside the door and peered at him with a knowing gaze. Those dark eyes were too shrewd and Noah felt himself squirm under their power.

Noah couldn't possibly tell this virtual stranger his twisted life story, so he decided to take the easy route and not say anything at all. The last thing he needed to do was lie to the first friend he'd made in town.

"I guess a man's business is his own." She touched his shoulder briefly. "I left home for a good reason too, at least it was a good reason at the time. Nowadays I'm not so sure."

Noah's mouth opened as if it was going to blurt out the truth, then the moment was broken by a bell ringing on the restaurant door.

"Marina, if you're comin' inside, then get on with it. You're blocking the door." An older woman with corkscrew silvery curls and a mustachioed upper lip poked her head out the door, frowning at both of them. "Don't hog the new sheriff now. Get on in here."

"You heard her. Let's get inside." Marina led him through the door, and Noah wondered what he'd gotten himself into.

Inside the restaurant, about two dozen eyes turned to look at Noah. He nodded and kept walking. Marina held his arm tight, giving him silent support. They sat at a table near the window where the petite curmudgeon met them.

"I'm Elsa." She held out her hand and Noah tried to shake it lightly. She wouldn't let him. With a grip that rivaled a bear trap, Elsa gave Noah her own bone-crunching version of howdy.

"Pleased to meet you, Miss Elsa. Noah Calhoun." He wondered if Elsa was friend or foe. He hoped it was friend because the little woman was formidable and he'd only known her a minute.

"I know who you are. Johnny's already been by. Glad to see a young strapping man take over the sheriffin' in this town. Been a couple years since Johnny's gun shot straight if ya know what I mean." She cackled, and her face lit with true humor. "Now sit down and I'll get y'all meatloaf and taters."

She walked away and Noah turned his gaze to Marina, who was smiling.

"Elsa takes some getting used to, but she means well." Marina laced her fingers together on the table. "I've never met anyone with a bigger heart in my life."

"She's quite a lady," Noah mused.

"Never meet a finer one. She's a damn good cook too."

Noah should have been shocked to hear a woman cussing, but since his mother had always indulged in the same habit, he couldn't fault Marina. His stomach rumbled and he hoped she was right about Elsa's cooking. The job was heaven-sent considering it included the food. Noah had spent a lot of time with a howling gut the last three years.

He felt the eyes on him. Each person in the room was judging him, sizing him up, fitting him for the position of protecting their town. He wasn't sure if he could do it, but he'd be damned if he'd let strangers' opinions dictate to him.

Before he could talk himself out of it, Noah stood and took off his hat.

"Folks, I'm sure y'all have heard that Johnny Boyton asked me to step into his shoes as the sheriff of Chancetown." He cleared his throat and willed away the jitters in his stomach. "I'm willing to do the best I can. I hope you can do the same for me. I'm not married, not looking for a wife, but I come from a good family. Um, thank you."

He sat down and met Marina's surprised gaze. "Bravo."

Noah fought the hunched shoulders that threatened. "I figure it's best to get it out of the way. Now we'll see if they can accept me."

He'd battled most of his life against things these good people couldn't even imagine. The Calhouns had given him a fresh start at fifteen. He'd always wanted to pay that back the best he could. Perhaps now was his opportunity.

৪১

Rosalyn Benedict knew good slops from bad ones. Elsa's restaurant definitely had the good eats. It had been her favorite place for a long time. She had a feeling Elsa deliberately put real food in with the slops, but Rosalyn wasn't going to complain. She ate enough each day to survive, and for that she was grateful. Since it was nearly time to eat, her stomach rumbled with hunger.

She waited in the shadows of the alley, content to listen to folks talking, the clink of forks on tin plates and the hooves of the horses on the street. Her cat, Whiskers, meowed at her feet as if to ask where the food was. Her warm fur swished against Rosalyn's leg. With a smile, she scratched the calico behind the ears.

"Don't worry, girl, we'll be eating soon. Why don't you go find yourself a juicy mouse?" Rosalyn felt the cat's purr through her skin. "Go on now."

Calling Whiskers "her" cat wasn't entirely true. No one owned the cat; she sort of adopted Rosalyn ten years ago and they'd been sleeping companions ever since. With one final meow, the cat disappeared into the sunshine streaming in at the end of the alley.

The door opened and Rosalyn shrank behind the empty crates. Silent as the cat she counted as her only friend, she didn't make a sound until the back door closed again. The scent of mashed potatoes and meatloaf tickled her nose.

She waited a full ten minutes, individually counting six hundred seconds before she moved. Even then, she advanced slowly on the bucket. No one else appeared and Rosalyn smiled at the feast. Meatloaf was her favorite.

After pulling her oft-washed handkerchief from her bag, she wiped her hands. As she peered into the bucket trying to decide on the choicest pieces of meat, a hand clamped down on her wrist.

Rosalyn looked up into the warmest pair of brown eyes she'd ever seen. They were attached to a man, a *stranger* with a strong grip, wavy brown hair and a gleaming silver star on his blue shirt.

"Let me go." She yanked, but he didn't move. In fact, he felt like an immovable rock.

"Ma'am, can I help you?"

Rosalyn frowned. "I don't need help and I sure as hell don't want any. Let me go." She pulled again and he budged only half an inch.

"I'm the new sheriff, Noah Calhoun." He looked down at the slops bucket with a look of pity. "You don't need to eat scraps from other people. Please let me help you."

"No." She couldn't be clearer than that. Was he touched in the head?

"Ma'am, I can't go about my business knowing you're eating slops and"—he glanced at her clothing—"from the look of you, living on the street."

"Where I live is none of your business."

He frowned. "It's my business now. Every person who lives in this town is my business."

"Well I ain't one of them." She tried to step on his foot, but he moved so quickly, even she was surprised. He had the grace of a big cat.

"I just want to help you." His grip didn't loosen, and no matter how much she yanked, she couldn't get her arm free.

Rosalyn sighed. "I don't want your help. Are you dense or something?"

The sheriff started to pull her toward the street. From there, she knew he'd take her to some woman who would force her to bathe, burn her clothes and say enough prayers to make her eyes cross.

Nothing doing.

Rosalyn opened her mouth and belted out a bloodcurdling scream. His eyes widened in shock and his grip loosened. That was all the opportunity she needed. She kicked him in the shin, got her arm free and ran down the alley toward the street, all too aware of the boots following hot on her heels.

"Ma'am, please wait."

No way Rosalyn was getting involved with the likes of the new sheriff. The townsfolk had tried it once, some church ladies who made her feel dirty and worthless. She might not have a place to sleep but she wasn't stupid or less than anyone else. Rosalyn had survived too long on her own to accept feeling less than human from anyone, no matter their intentions.

She turned the corner and nearly knocked over some woman who squawked like a chicken. Rosalyn knew she hadn't done any harm, so she kept running. Sheriff Calhoun wasn't so lucky. A grunt and another squawk told her the man had run into the biddy. Good. That would slow him down enough for Rosalyn to get away.

After ten minutes and a lot of doubling back, Rosalyn made it to her favorite sleeping area. The back stairs of Marina's saloon had a cozy spot beneath them, perfect for one woman and a cat. Whiskers sat atop the blanket Rosalyn had rescued from the trash pile outside the hotel. It had a burn hole in it likely from some fella's cigar, but it was a nice wool blanket that kept her warm in the winter.

Whiskers licked her chops and watched with her wise golden eyes. Rosalyn bent over with her hands on her knees and caught her breath, allowing the air to go deep before she let it out slowly.

"There's a new sheriff in town." Rosalyn shook her head. "I expect he'll do his best to catch me for a bit so we'll need to be smart."

She picked up the cat and scooted under the stairs. After settling onto the blanket, she put Whiskers on her lap, grateful for the cat's comforting warmth.

"Noah. He said his name was Noah."

His eyes had been an unusual shade of brown, almost like fine whiskey. The left one also had a dark spot in it, like a freckle. A scar bisected one eyebrow while another decorated the corner of his lips.

Holy Mary.

How did she remember all that from seeing the man for one minute? Rosalyn had always been good with details, but this was beyond that. It was a little frightening.

Self-preservation kicked in and her mind scrabbled away from the memories of the too-handsome sheriff. A man like him might try to take advantage of a girl, using his good looks and sweetness.

Rosalyn couldn't afford to make *that* mistake again. One smooth-talking stranger was enough to last her a lifetime.

All she needed to do was stay away from him. Far away.

It took nearly five minutes to calm the woman down after he'd knocked her into the wall. Noah used every trick he'd learned from his charming Uncle Trevor to get out of a tough situation. After tipping his hat and saying good day, he was finally able to look for the woman from the alley.

At first he hadn't been sure it was a woman beneath the snarled black hair, but then he'd seen her face. A heart-shaped face with unusual violet eyes full of mistrust, pride and annoyance. However, there hadn't been any fear. Whoever she was, he hadn't scared her, which was good. He wanted to help her, not frighten her.

After a ten minute fruitless search, he found himself back at Elsa's and an amused-looking Marina.

"Where did you disappear to?"

"I found someone."

I found someone. The way it came out of his mouth jarred him a bit. Why didn't he say something different? Like, "There was a woman in the alley" or "I was trying to help someone in trouble". But no, instead he had to say that he found her.

Had he found her? She likely hadn't been lost. For all he knew, she had simply fallen on hard times for a bit.

"Really? Who did you find?" Marina turned toward the saloon and Noah fell into step beside her.

"A woman. She was about to eat from the slops bucket when I found her."

"Rosalyn Benedict." Marina shook her head. "Sweet kid."

"Kid? How old is she?" Noah was suddenly fascinated with Marina's answer, gripped with a burning need to know more about the mysterious woman named Rosalyn.

"I think she's about eighteen or so. She's lived on the streets for as long as I've been here, maybe ten years. Most folks pay her no mind." Marina glanced at him. "I think Elsa leaves her food and so does Jacob at the hotel. Folks try to take care of her, but she's skittish."

Noah remembered being hungry, begging for food, depending on others for everything. An ancient thrum of pain echoed through him. No matter how many nights he'd slept in a comfortable bed with a full belly, the fear of having nothing never left. Even as a grown man, that little boy existed deep within him, scared and alone. Rosalyn was a kindred spirit.

With a surge of hope, Noah found his first task as the sheriff of Chancetown. He was going to help Rosalyn Benedict.

Chapter Two

When he arrived back at the jail Noah sucked in a breath and the scent of lye and pine oil tickled his nose. Bitsy and Cherry might be a lot of things, but they were dang good cleaners. The jail probably hadn't been that clean when it was built. Even Johnny's dirty dishes were washed and stacked neatly on the table in the corner.

He sat at the desk, pleased to be able to call it "his" desk. Never thought that would happen.

"Calhoun?"

Noah looked up at the doorway to see a bald, portly man in a tight navy blue suit sporting a small dark mustache and a toothy grin.

"Yes, that's me." He stood, wondering why the man reminded him of a snake-oil salesman.

"Sylvester Dickinson. I'm the mayor of Chancetown." The man glanced around with a wide smile and sniffed. "It surely smells better in here than the last time I visited Johnny." His too-big grin brought to mind a wolf in sheep's clothing.

"I had it cleaned." Noah held out his hand. "Noah Calhoun."

Dickinson pumped Noah's proffered hand until he had to pull it back. This man's charm oozed out of each and every pore. His initial impression of a big predator hadn't been mistaken.

"I wanted to stop by and welcome you to Chancetown. Johnny tells me you are an excellent lawman, exactly what we need. Your salary will be paid by the town, by me actually. I wanted to warn you a bit about some pitfalls." Dickinson's smile didn't reach his eyes. "Some folks will try to take advantage of you."

"Well, I don't think—"

"Don't worry." Dickinson waved his hand in the air. "I don't expect you to think, just to work. Don't get in the middle of the sheep and cattle ranchers' battle. Eventually the sheepmen will be driven out or killed." Dickinson smiled again. "Do you understand?"

Killed? The mayor wanted sheep ranchers *killed?* "What are you saying, Mr. Dickinson?" Noah chose his words with care, his temper simmering.

"The town council doesn't want the battle. Never you mind any more than that. I own the bank and half the buildings on the east side of town, including this one. The town was built from the blood of cattle and there just isn't enough grazing land for sheep." He sat on the edge of the desk. "You've got the look of a cattleman to me." The blinding smile appeared again.

Noah took a deep breath, then let it out. He had to do it a second time to rein in the words that threatened to tumble from his mouth. No need to offend the mayor on his first day, but the man had some loco notions.

"I have worked cattle ranches, but my parents own a horse ranch."

"Ah, see, there you have it. A cattleman." Dickinson stood and straightened his jacket. "Do you have any questions for me?"

"I owe Bitsy and Cherry from the saloon for cleaning the jail." And he hoped to have enough to pay for a bath.

"Don't you worry. I'll take care of that debt for you." The lascivious grin made Noah's instincts stand at attention. Something wasn't right about the man and it wasn't just his too-white teeth.

"Anything else?" Dickinson's eyes appeared like the surface of a calm pond. Couldn't see much but a reflection, but Noah sensed there was a lot going on beneath.

"Is it possible to get a few dollars until payday? I'd like to get some laundry washed and perhaps a bath or two." Noah couldn't remember the last time he'd had a hot bath.

"Of course." Dickinson reached into his pocket and peeled off a few dollars from the fat wad of cash clutched in his hand.

Noah tucked the money into his pocket. "Much obliged, Mr. Dickinson."

"Good. If you have any questions, you come to me. Lots of gossips in this town like to fill your head with trash, but I know everything that goes on." He touched the brim of his hat. "I think we'll get along just fine."

"I'll do my best," Noah said with a forced smile.

"You do that." With another look around the jail, Dickinson turned to leave. "I swear I still smell Bitsy in here. She's quite a woman." He winked and took his bright smiling face from the building.

After the door closed on his visitor, Noah sat down with a gust of breath and a shake of his head. He didn't know exactly what was going on in Chancetown, but after his conversation with the mayor, it wasn't good. There was apparently a feud going on and he expected to be in the middle of it. Good thing his father had taught him how to survive. He'd need all his wits and skills to be razor-sharp.

Rosalyn waited until dusk to wash. After hiding from the sheriff in lots of places that hadn't ever seen either end of a scrub brush, she needed to get the grime off her hands. She was so hungry her stomach nearly rubbed on her backbone, but she wanted to wait to be sure that sheriff wasn't around. He'd forced her to miss dinner. She'd be damned if she'd let him make her miss supper too.

The horse trough in front of the post office was the cleanest, but it was right next to the jail. She bit her lip, arguing with herself for a good hour on whether or not to do it. When the noise in the street settled down on the north end, and most folks were at the south end in the saloons and restaurants, Rosalyn emerged.

Whiskers stuck to her side like an attack cat. She would've smiled if she hadn't been so annoyed at the whole prospect of hiding from the man. It wasn't as if he'd threatened her, or at least not with anything but polite concern, yet Rosalyn was still unsettled. She didn't know if it was from her reaction to the man or something he'd done, but she followed her instincts. They were crying danger.

Dipping her tin cup into the trough, she set it aside to rinse. With the sliver of soap from her washrag, she soaped up her hands. Of course, her gaze strayed to the jail and she wondered if he was in there and what he was doing. She shouldn't be thinking about the man, but there he was like a ghostie in her brain.

As if she'd conjured him, he stepped out of the jail into the fading sunlight. The orange glow from the sunset bathed him, turning his brown hair into a fiery halo. She stopped in mid-wash to stare, every small hair on her body standing on end. Her heart thundered, blood pumping past her ears until she could hear nothing but the rhythm of her body.

She'd never experienced anything like it. Before she could even think about running, he spotted her and smiled.

Shit.

The man smiled like an angel from heaven above. Rosalyn's feet were rooted to the ground, helpless as he walked toward her, a lean-hipped swagger that reminded her again of a big brown cat. He took off his hat and nodded. Her body had taken control and refused to budge an inch even as her head screamed at her to run.

"Good evening, Rosalyn."

Well, now he knew her name. She wondered who'd snitched on her.

"I told you to leave me alone. Are you deaf or just stupid?" Her heated reaction was part annoyance, part arousal. Seeing the handsome man with the whiskey eyes did something to her no man had ever done—made her lose control. Whiskers meowed noisily at her feet.

"Neither, ma'am. I'm just trying to do the right thing." He glanced at the soap in her hand. "Can I offer you some supper?"

Rosalyn's heart slammed against her chest in anger and disappointment. Her temporary lunacy broke like a bubble. How dare he? She wasn't a charity case to throw food at because he wanted to feel good about himself. After rinsing her hands with the tin cup of clean water, she wiped them on her handkerchief and walked toward him.

A look of puzzlement drifted across his features before he smiled again. Rosalyn smiled back then pushed him in the horse trough. He landed with a huge splash, spraying water every which way. The look on his face, however, sent her into peals of laugher. Shock, surprise and bewilderment. It had probably been years since anyone had taken advantage of the tough sheriff.

Unfortunately, Rosalyn forgot just how fast he moved. Within seconds, he was back on his feet and coming straight at her. Her hesitation cost her plenty because he got a hold on her arm, a tight grip that told her the surprise from the dunking was over. Sheriff Calhoun was angry.

Whiskers was nowhere to be found, but Rosalyn didn't blame the cat. She tried to twist away but his hold was too strong. Before she could utter a protest, she was immersed in the horse trough. The cold water shocked her so much she left her mouth open and a gush of it slid down her throat. She choked and sputtered, trying desperately to crawl out of the water.

He hauled her out of the trough as quickly as he'd thrown her in. She flopped onto his shoulder, stomach down, and the water in her throat ended up on his backside. If she wasn't gasping for air, she'd have laughed at the sight.

The sheriff spanked her behind once. "That wasn't very nice, Rosalyn." He stomped into the jail, slamming the door behind him.

A shiver of fear ran down her back and she struggled against him. Just because he was sheriff didn't mean he wouldn't throw her on the mattress and stick his prick in her. She'd promised herself years ago to protect herself from any and all men.

"Relax, little one. I'm not going to hurt you." His voice echoed with sincerity, yet Rosalyn couldn't stop the panic.

He set her on her feet and stepped back, closing the cell door in her face. Rosalyn gaped at the bars, then at him. He'd lost his hat somewhere along the way and his wavy brown hair hung in wet strands down his cheeks. A bit of green slime from the trough stuck to his jaw and she had the mad urge to wipe it off.

"What are you doing? Let me out of here." Rosalyn touched the cold metal bars and shivered.

"You just assaulted an officer of the law, therefore, you broke the law. I'm within my rights to arrest you." He put his hands on his hips and glared. "You had no call to push me in that trough."

"You did the same to me." Rosalyn didn't mean to sound petulant, it just happened.

"No, I didn't. I dunked you to teach you a lesson." He pointed at the bars. "Just as this is meant to teach you a lesson. My pa believes the hardest lessons are the ones we remember the best."

Rosalyn swallowed the tang of the water on her tongue. "I learned my lesson, now let me out."

"You can stay here for tonight. I won't let anyone else in here so don't worry about that." He swiped his hand down his face. "In the meantime, I'm going upstairs to get you a towel. I don't suppose you have another set of clothes?"

"You can't be serious." Rosalyn's anger kicked aside her apprehension.

"Oh, I'm serious." He turned away, heading for the stairs at the end of the room. "Be right back."

Rosalyn listened to his boots on the stairs, followed by a squishy sound from the water within them. She stuck her tongue out at the empty space. "Ha! That'll teach you."

She yanked on the bars, rattling the door within its hinges. Of course, a little rattle did not mean it was going to open. She pulled harder and only succeeded in almost wrenching her arms from their sockets. By the time he came back a minute later with a towel, she had worked up a good fit.

He handed her the towel between the bars and she grabbed it hard, knocking him off balance. His shoulder bumped into the bars and he grunted. Rosalyn smiled and tugged harder. When he tugged back, the bars were suddenly in front of her nose. His hand was the only thing that stopped her from bloodying it.

"Don't try that again, little one. I won't be so nice next time." His gaze told her that what he said, he meant.

Rosalyn spat the taste of the water on the floor. "You don't scare me, *Sheriff*. I've survived harder men than you."

Regardless of his plans for her, Rosalyn wasn't about to allow him to cow her. It was too important to let him know that he couldn't, rather than he shouldn't.

The sheriff glanced down at her spit, then dropped the towel on it. "I guess you ought to get cleaned up then."

When he turned away, she growled and stomped her foot. How did a simple act turn into a temper tantrum from a jail?

"After I change I'm going to get us some supper from Elsa. I suggest you dry yourself off while I'm gone. I'll lock the door so no one comes in to bother you." His voice was full of tightly controlled annoyance and something that might be respect.

Or at least she thought that's what it was. She hadn't been around people enough to be able to read them exactly, but what she did know let her believe that Calhoun meant what he said. He was teaching her a lesson. Too bad Rosalyn didn't want to be his pupil.

Noah clenched his shaking hands into fists so Rosalyn wouldn't see how much she affected him. He ran up the steps and dug around in his saddlebags for his second set of clothes. He shed the sodden ones, and they plopped to the floor. How had things gotten so out of control in a breath of a moment?

He only wanted to talk to her to find out who she was and why she lived on the streets of Chancetown. When she pushed him in that trough, Noah was overtaken, awash in emotions that he didn't know what to do with. He'd been battered by deep anger, a thirst for revenge and raging passion, as if Rosalyn had reached in and pulled it all out of him. Suddenly there he was, dunking her in the water and throwing her in the jail cell. What had possessed him?

Growing up under the thumb of an evil man had taught Noah how to be small, to be unseen. Living with his adoptive parents for six years had brought him forward but not completely out of the four walls he'd built around himself so long ago. With one twitch of her mouth and a laugh that would likely haunt his dreams for weeks, Rosalyn laid siege to those walls.

Noah had nothing to towel off with since he'd given her the threadbare one he had. He used his clean shirt to blot the water. He'd find the bathing house another time. He was sure Marina knew who he could pay to do his laundry and where to take a bath—two things he really needed to do. With Mayor Dickinson watching his every move and rumored sheep and cattle rancher problems, the job that had seemed like a dream, an easy solution to a tough problem, was going to be harder than he'd ever anticipated.

When Noah left home three years ago, his mother asked him not to go. She didn't beg, or tell, she just looked at him with those green eyes and asked. Noah hadn't been able to stay. He was grateful to the Calhouns and Malloys for all the love and family they gave him. Something he'd never had, even from his own mother who'd died when he was twelve. Nicky had given him love and the confidence to be who he was. Tyler had given him the skills to survive. Together they had given an orphan a home and a new life.

Noah pulled on his dry clothes, wondering why, now, he was so melancholy about leaving home. It had been three years and he thought he'd be over the sadness, the ache of wanting to see his family again. His little sisters and brother, the cousins and aunts and uncles and grandparents. He shook his head to clear it. Getting maudlin while he had a woman locked up in his jail cell was not a good idea.

He dumped the water out of his boots the best he could and left the sodden pile of clothes for later. He grabbed his soap from the saddlebags as well as a chipped pitcher of water from the dresser in the room. As he walked downstairs, he braced himself for another confrontation with Rosalyn. She stood where he'd left her, arms crossed, violet eyes flashing. Her tangled black hair fell in wild waves around her heart-shaped face. The shapeless brown rag that passed as a dress clung to every bit of her body.

Noah had been too angry to notice that Rosalyn was definitely not a young girl. She was a woman, all woman, with gentle curves and full breasts his hands twitched to trace. His confusion was kicked aside by the passion that again surged inside him. It seemed ridiculous to feel such intensity for a woman who lived on the streets, who'd probably like nothing more than to never see him again.

His blood thrummed through his veins, and his balls grew heavy as tingles raced up and down his hardening staff. She must've seen something in his eyes because her angry gaze turned wary and she stepped back, her arms in a protective pose.

"I ain't giving you nothing."

Noah shook his head. "I'm not asking you for anything."

"You lie. I see it in your eyes, Sheriff." She glanced at his trousers. "Oh, you definitely lie."

Noah stepped closer. He could see her tremble as if forcing herself to stay put, to not be intimidated by him.

"I won't hurt you, Rosalyn. I promise." He moved even closer. "You might want to dry off. It still gets pretty chilly at night."

He hoped to do more than scare her and throw her in a jail cell, but unless she was willing to let him, he couldn't. The last thing he wanted was to force Rosalyn into letting him help her. She was a person and deserved more respect than that, but she also couldn't go around pushing the town sheriff into a trough on his first day.

Noah knew about appearances and what people thought. He'd lose credibility if there were no consequences. What he was doing to her wasn't exactly punishment, he was helping her. He had to keep repeating that to himself, then perhaps he might believe it.

He reached through the bars and set the pitcher and soap on the floor next to the towel. "I'm leaving to get supper and see about getting you some dry things."

"Don't you dare." Her anger ballooned into a threat.

"Dare what?"

"I don't need your charity, Sheriff."

"Call me Noah."

"I don't need your charity, Noah," she repeated. "You let me out of this cell and I'll go get my own dry clothes."

"Sorry, I can't do that. You broke the law. For that, you're going to spend the night in here."

She bared her teeth in a snarl. Noah reacted like a dog scenting a bitch in heat. He stood straighter, trembling with the force of the blood rushing around in his veins. Their gazes locked.

"I hate you." The venom in her voice was enough for three snakes.

Noah flinched. "I'm sorry to hear that because I really only want to help you."

Rosalyn strode forward and gripped the bars, narrowing her gaze. "You're a liar. If you wanted to help me you wouldn't keep me locked up in here. You think just because you're a man that you can do whatever you want. Just look out, Sheriff Noah. Soon as your back is turned, I'll be gone so fast you'll never catch me."

Noah believed every word of it. She didn't want his help and from what she said, she didn't need his help. He was going to give it to her whether she objected or not.

Chapter Three

Rosalyn shivered in the cold cell, cursing herself for wishing the sheriff would hurry back with dry clothes. She'd told him she didn't want dry clothes, but she'd also bet a week's worth of Elsa's slops that he brought them anyway.

Noah.

His name invoked wishes a woman like her should never have. That man would never want someone who lived in an alley with only a cat for company. She'd done some terrible things to survive, things even she didn't want to think about. A man like him probably would turn away in disgust from her if he knew the truth.

Better to keep him at a distance than to allow him to get any closer. Rosalyn was no fool; she refused to risk her heart for any man, even if his brown eyes were burned into her memory.

She leaned her head on the bars and sighed. Pushing him in the trough had been a mistake. She acknowledged that now, however, it was too late to turn back time. Apparently Noah didn't like to be toyed with, even if it had been pretty dang funny. Dunking her in the water had been a surprise, not to say she hadn't deserved it, but she certainly hadn't liked it.

The scrape of the door startled her and she jumped about a foot in the air. Fortunately for her, he was looking down, so he didn't see her silly reaction. When he shut the door behind him, the aroma of fresh bread and some kind of meat wafted toward her.

Rosalyn's mouth watered at the smell and the sight of Noah walking toward her with a paper-wrapped package and a heaping plate of food.

He eyed her. "If I give you the food, are you going to throw it? If you are, let me know now because I don't want to waste these pork chops and gravy."

Pork chops. Oh Lord, her favorite.

"No, I swear I won't." Her stomach rumbled loud enough to rattle the windows.

A grin played around his mouth. "I think I believe you."

He set the package down and fished the keys out of his pocket. When the tumbler scraped in the lock, he looked her in the eye. The door swung wide. This was her chance, the opportunity to throw the hot food in his face and run. He knew it too. The wariness in his eyes battled with a big dollop of hope.

For some reason, this man wanted to help her. She had no idea why or what he'd get from it, but the earnestness in his face couldn't be mistaken. Could it be he was a genuine person? An honest person?

In her experience most men were dishonest. Rosalyn promised herself she'd find out his real reasons for helping her, but her hunger overcame her need for the truth. She sat on the cot and waited.

Noah's brows shot toward his hairline when she gave in, but he didn't say a word. Instead he pulled an empty plate from beneath the full one and handed it to her along with a fork from his pocket. Then he kneeled on the floor and offered her the first pass at the food.

A stupid lump formed in her throat at the gesture. Not only was the sheriff being kind to her after she'd humiliated him, but he'd brought her the first true meal she'd had in so long she couldn't remember it. A welling of respect and a grudging friendliness hit her.

She used the fork to grab half the mashed potatoes and a pork chop, then a passel of peas and a hunk of bread. It smelled heavenly and it was really hot. Not the lukewarm hot she was used to. She dug into the peas and shoved a forkful in her mouth. The butter and the sweet taste of the vegetable coated her tongue. With a moan of pleasure, she took another huge mouthful and closed her eyes in sheer delight.

"Good peas?"

She opened one eye to glare at him, still kneeling and looking at her with amusement. "Get up and eat your own food. Quit staring at me. It ain't polite."

"No, it *isn't* polite."

"You gonna correct my speech now too?" she grumped.

"My mama did until she cured me of my poor schooling." He sat cross-legged on the floor with the plate in his lap. "Eventually it became second nature to speak correctly."

"Why did you have poor schooling if your mama was smart like that?" A heaping forkful of potatoes went down easily after the peas.

"My real mama wasn't schooled. It was the folks who adopted me who taught me." He didn't meet her gaze and Rosalyn decided he didn't really want to talk about it.

Noah ate like a gentleman, alternately using his fork to take human-sized bites, and wiping his mouth with a handkerchief he'd laid on his leg. She didn't know whether to be surprised by the fact that he sat on the floor to eat with her or that he chose to eat with her.

Rosalyn hadn't had company for her meals other than Whiskers in many years. It felt odd to eat with another person.

He had beautiful teeth, straight and a nice shade of white. He focused on his food, seeming to allow her to peruse him and what he was doing. She started eating her pork chop, when her curiosity finally got the best of her.

"You're not from around here."

He glanced up. "No."

She took a bite before asking another question. "So where are you from?"

"Curious about me, Rosalyn?" he teased.

"Well, yes."

He laughed with that rich, deep sound that made her feel funny inside. She realized it was the urge to laugh with him. It shocked her enough that she dropped the pork chop right into the mashed potatoes, which splattered on her leg. It wasn't hot enough to burn so she used her finger to scoop it up and stick it in her mouth.

When she looked up at him, he was holding out a handkerchief. "This is a clean one, I swear."

The fabric was soft, certainly softer than her own pitiful handkerchief, which was likely a soggy mess in her pocket. His was not new, but it was a high quality piece of fabric.

"Thank you," she grudgingly said, recognizing he'd skirted the question about where he was from quite nicely.

"You're welcome."

He went back to eating his dinner as if they were sitting in a fancy restaurant instead of in a jail cell, although both of them still showed evidence of a dunking in the trough. Suddenly it all struck her as funny and a chuckle escaped like a burp.

"Was it something I said?" His fork paused in midair.

Another chuckle leaked out. She shook her head, afraid if she tried to speak she really would laugh. He shrugged and ate again. In ten minutes both of them had cleared their plates. The only things remaining were the remnants of the pork chops, gnawed and nibbled until nothing was left but the bones.

He stood and held out his hand. She shrank back from him, knowing now he'd want his payment.

"Your plate, Rosalyn. All I want is your plate. I have to bring them back to Elsa."

Rosalyn's cheeks heated. No matter how nice the sheriff was, she would always be on her guard. That didn't mean she couldn't be embarrassed by her reactions. After she handed him the plate without a word, he stacked them together and stepped out of the cell. Rosalyn waited for the clang of the door and key turning in the lock.

It didn't happen.

Instead, he reached down and set the brown-paper-wrapped package on the cot next to her.

"You're about the same size as my Aunt Lily so I got something that would fit her."

She looked at the package, her fingers itching to untie the twine bow at the top. It had been quite some time since Rosalyn had opened a package, even longer since someone had given her a gift. Somewhere deep inside her a tiny flame of hope lit against her wishes. If she wasn't careful, Noah Calhoun could completely turn her life upside down.

"I'm going to leave you alone so you can change. The towel, soap and water are there for you to use."

She finally turned her gaze to his and saw sincerity, honesty and a pulse from a kindred spirit. That's when she knew Noah had not always been a well-taken-care-of man. She'd bet every penny she had, which totaled twenty-eight cents, that Noah was more like her, had experienced similar things. She didn't know why she thought that, but it rang true.

"I'm not going to lock you up, but I will offer you the use of the cell anytime you want. I'll even let you hold the keys if that makes you feel safer. I just want to help you, Rosalyn. I hope you can believe that."

He turned and left her alone, leaving the cell door wide open, the keys dangling from the lock.

"Wait," Rosalyn called.

Noah paused in mid-stride. "What's the matter?"

"I can't take this." She stepped out of the cell and thrust the brown paper package toward him. "I don't take charity."

She'd almost accepted it without question, now he'd have to convince her to. He wouldn't be able to live with himself if he didn't help her.

"Okay, so it's not charity. You can work for it." The moment the words left his mouth, he realized he chose the wrong ones.

Her gaze narrowed. "I knew there'd be something like that in there."

"Not like that. I meant you could clean, keep the jail tidy."

She sniffed. "Smells like it's already been cleaned."

"You're right. It was cleaned today but it will get dirty again. It's a jail, lots of folks tromping in and out of here, bringing in mud and dirt. I'm sure there's going to be at least one or two drunks in the other cell. I'm offering you a job."

Another one of those bell-tinkling laughs popped out of her mouth, the ones that made his stomach clench and his blood thrum.

"Is that funny?"

She pulled the brown paper package to her chest and crossed her arms over it. "I was just thinking of myself as a deputy."

Noah smiled. "Then that's what you'll be."

Shock blazed across her face. "I was just fooling with you."

Noah knew Mayor Dickinson would not approve of a female deputy, much less the woman who lived in the streets of his fair town. However, he didn't need to know.

"Well, I'm not. That old fool sheriff left quite a mess here. I'm not just talking about dirt. There's piles of papers and wanted posters. I don't think he spent a whole lot of time taking care of the details." He pointed at the package. "Why don't you get changed, then you and I can talk about it." He left her alone in the jail to think about the proposal.

The longer he thought about Rosalyn being his deputy, the more the idea appealed to him. She reminded him a bit of his adopted mother, with her toughness, her savvy, her ability to land on her feet and come up swinging. Rosalyn was a beautiful, sexy woman, a force to be reckoned with. Maybe all she needed was a chance. Noah could give that to her.

∞

It was well past dark before he came back to the jail. As he tiptoed past the cell, he couldn't help but glance in, hoping she'd be there. The moonlight streamed through the small window, bathing her body in its silvery glow. The keys were firmly clenched in her hand—no doubt the cell was locked up tight, protecting her. When his gaze arrived at her face, he wasn't surprised to find her staring at him.

"I'm only staying here because it's late and I'm tired. I ain't gonna be here when you wake up."

Noah nodded. "That's your choice." He took a deep breath, swallowing the rest of the words dancing on his tongue. What he really wanted to do was find out why she stayed, why she needed to lock herself in and why she couldn't be there when he woke up.

Her eyes were as dark as pitch in the shadowed cell. He wished he could see them so he'd know what she was thinking.

"There ain't no second set of keys is there?"

He chuckled. "Not as far as I know. That's the only set. So don't lose them, okay?"

"You can believe ain't nobody taking these from me." She shifted positions on the cot. "The ground is more comfortable than this thing. You ought to look into replacing these."

"I'll do that. Believe me, I know the feeling of sleeping on an uncomfortable cot in a jail cell. Good night, Rosalyn."

"G'night, Sheriff."

As Noah walked up the stairs, her even breathing reminded him that for the first time in a long time, he wasn't alone.

∽

The next morning the cell was empty, the door standing wide open. Noah combated his disappointment by stepping outside and walking around for half an hour, nodding and chatting with folks. It was just what he needed to feel at least a smidge better, if not less lonely. When he stopped in the General Store, the owner's wife, a blonde, rotund, apple-cheeked woman named Helga Knudsen, greeted him warmly. He'd met her husband the day before when he'd purchased the dress for Rosalyn. It was the first time he'd ever purchased anything on credit—the urge to pay off his account niggled at him. Just putting his name on the books made his skin jump. However, he'd done it, and he'd done it for someone he barely knew.

"You are living at the jail, ya?" She handed him a slice of strudel wrapped in a piece of wax paper.

He eyed the sweet apple-raisin concoction with no small amount of delight. "Yes, in the room above the jail."

She shook her head and tsked. "Too bad. You should find yourself a wife. My daughter, Josephine, is sixteen, and a lovely cook."

Noah smiled and thought about how he could escape without offending Mrs. Knudsen. "Thank you for the strudel, ma'am. Is there anything as sheriff I can do to help you or your husband?"

"Such a nice boy." She reached up and patted his cheek. "We have a couple people who don't pay on their account, but no trouble. I will be sure to stop by with Josephine to say hello."

Noah thanked her again and politely took his leave. Outside, he marveled at a matchmaking mama after him in less than two days. He considered eating the strudel but his appetite had been absent, gone apparently with a violet-eyed waif.

When he stepped back into the jail, his eyes widened and his mouth dropped open. In the short amount of time he was walking around and talking to Mrs. Knudsen, Rosalyn had come back to the jail. She'd taken each piece of paper from the sheriff's piles on the desk and scattered them around the room. Every square inch of floor had a piece of paper on it. When he slammed the door, the force of the wind made them all flutter like a wild swarm of moths.

"What are you doing?" He dropped the wrapped strudel on the floor, forgetting the fact he was glad to see her.

Rosalyn sat in the middle of all of it in the dark blue dress he'd bought for her. He was momentarily distracted by the sight of her wearing a form-fitting dress that cupped her full breasts and displayed her curves. They'd more than tempt a man.

Then he remembered what she'd done. Anger pulsed through him. He'd offered to help her, even fed her and bought her a damn dress and how did she pay him back? By making an even bigger mess.

"Don't step on that one," she scolded.

"What are you doing?" he repeated, a little more loudly.

"You don't need to shout. I'm sitting two feet away from you." She rubbed one ear and frowned. "I'm not a very good reader, but from what I can tell, there's about twenty-seven kinds of papers here. Some of them are wanted posters. That's one word I can read. I left those on the desk. The other twenty-six different kinds, I can't rightly tell what a lot of them are. I spread them all out so I could sort them into piles for you."

His anger deflated. She was helping him?

"I, uh..."

Rosalyn stood, putting her hands on her hips, her black curls swinging. "You said you was gonna give me a job and that I could keep this place clean. Well, I started by cleaning up the papers." She spread her arms wide. "I ain't never had so much space to work with and it just made it easier to try to figure out what the papers were. Until you came in here and started shouting like a madman."

He stepped toward her. "I'm sorry."

She moved back. "You ought to be. You were rude."

Noah took another step and she frowned harder. For a moment there, he forgot what they were even arguing about. Her brows knitted together, and the crease between them begged for a kiss to smooth it away. She'd used the soap he'd left for her, and the smell of freshly scrubbed skin drifted past him, a clean scent that appealed to him. As a young man, he hadn't taken many baths since there hadn't been much of an option for a warm one. Now, he loved taking a bath. The hotter the better.

Long, soaking baths were his favorite. The image of Rosalyn in the bathtub danced across his mind. He shut his eyes to block it out. This after she'd simply washed her face and hands. He wasn't sure it was such a good idea to have her there all the time, if this was his reaction. However he'd made the offer and he wasn't about to rescind it.

When he opened his eyes, she was headed toward the door, her nose in the air. She scooped up the strudel and sniffed.

"Rosalyn, wait, please."

She stopped, her hand on the doorknob. "You don't want me here."

"That's not true." He took a deep breath. "I was just surprised, that's all. It's been an interesting first two days on the job."

"Two days? You've only been doing this two days?" Both dark eyebrows shot toward the ceiling.

"Sheriff Boyton hired me yesterday morning. So today is my second day as sheriff."

She shrugged. "We all make mistakes when we try something for the first time. Ain't never been a sheriff before, have you?"

"No, I haven't been a sheriff before." He examined the calluses on his hands rather than look her in the eye. Noah had been many things over the course of his life. This was the first time he was doing something that could really make a difference in people's lives. He'd been opposed to the idea when the sheriff suggested it, but now that he was here with the star on his chest and the power in his hands, he could make that difference. He'd have to use his other skills to handle the town's problems and the mayor.

"Will you stay?" He got those three words out, unaccountably hoping she'd say yes, stupidly wanting to add "always" to the question.

"If you keep your hands to yourself, yes, I'll stay, but just for a little while. I don't know how long I'm going to be here. I guess it's time I tried something new." She held up the strudel. "Is this for me?"

Noah smiled and wonder of wonders, Rosalyn smiled back. His fragile heart that he kept in a safe place quivered at the sight of that smile. He wondered just how much his new deputy would change his life.

Chapter Four

"I ain't taking no bath." Rosalyn stuck up her chin at the too-tall sheriff. "I already washed up good. You've been near me two days now, do I smell?"

He loomed over her. "You washed your face and hands with a pitcher of water and a sliver of soap I gave you. That's not washing up good." He took hold of her arm and slid the sleeve back, pointing at the dirt beneath. "You need a bath." Noah pronounced each word like he was talking to an idiot.

She snatched her arm away. "I said I ain't taking no bath and you can't make me."

"No, you're right, I can't. But a sheriff's deputy can't go around with enough dirt stuck on her body to make an ant hill. No one is going to hurt you, Rosalyn, I promise. We'll go down to that bathing house down the street. Marina said they were good. I'll make sure you have privacy and that no one bothers you."

Her heart went clippity-clop at the thought that he'd be there watching over her, or perhaps watching her. Was that a good thing or a bad thing? Her body and her mind were all mixed up about Noah Calhoun.

"The lady who owns that bathing house don't like me." Her words were a little less forceful as she wavered on her decision to refuse a bath.

"I don't care if she doesn't like you. I do."

That statement made every small hair on her body stand up.

Rosalyn's resolve weakened again. "I just can't pour that cold water all over me."

"It won't be cold. They heat the water."

The idea of a warm bath hadn't occurred to her because when she did take a bath and wash up all over, she did it in the creek right outside town. That water was always cold, sometimes colder than cold. "A warm bath?"

He grinned. "Possibly even hot."

"Well, if it's warm enough for me, I might take a bath. I ain't saying that I'm gonna do it, I'm just saying that I'll walk down there with you."

"Sounds good. Thank you, Rosalyn."

He held out his arm and she stared at it, unsure and awkward. She didn't know how to walk with a gentleman. Lord have mercy, she was no lady.

"Take your arm and put it through mine like this." Noah took hold of her arm and tucked it around his until her hand rested on his forearm. "It's not hard. Are you ready?"

His scent, a combination of man, good old-fashioned sweat and something else she suspected was unique to Noah Calhoun, teased her nose. Not to mention, his presence next to her comforted her somehow. Her insides quivered and she hoped he didn't notice. That would be really embarrassing.

"It still don't mean that I'm gonna lay on my back for you."

Noah's eyes registered surprise, then disappointment. "I never expected that from you, Rosalyn, and I wouldn't take it from you."

She'd mucked up the moment, the sweet moment of him treating her like a lady, but it didn't matter. None of it mattered. This was all like a story, one of those tales parents told their young'uns. Only it probably wouldn't have a happy ending.

They walked down to the bathing house together, arm in arm. A few heads turned as they passed by. She'd hazard a guess that most folks noticed, and surprisingly some paid them no mind. The bathing house had a fancy sign out in front with swirly gold letters. Although she couldn't read what it said, Rosalyn knew her ABCs. It was just a matter of putting them together to make words that she had trouble with. Still she knew this was the bathing house and that awful woman with the doughy face and the big flappy arms owned it. She'd chased Rosalyn away from behind the building lots of times. She must have trembled or shivered or something, because Noah laid his hand on top of hers and squeezed.

"I won't let her hurt you. It'll be okay."

Stupid as it sounded, his reassurance actually made her feel better. It was odd and a little frightening. Rosalyn reminded herself that the sheriff was helping her because he wanted to feel good about himself, not because he cared about her.

When they stepped into the bathing house, Rosalyn's stomach got tight and she braced herself. It was a good thing too. The owner rose from her stool in the corner, planting fleshy fists on her ample hips.

"That thing is not welcome in here."

To his credit, Noah took off his hat like a gentleman. "Ma'am. I'm Noah Calhoun, the new sheriff."

She pointed at Rosalyn. "She's got to go. I don't give no charity."

Noah's muscles tensed beneath Rosalyn's hand. "Miss Benedict is my guest and deserves some courtesy. May I have your name please?"

His politeness impressed Rosalyn. She'd have started cussing right about then.

"Clara Cartman." The older woman shook her head, the rolls on her neck moving on their own. "You shouldn't be with her type. Folks won't take kindly to it."

"I expect our citizens to be kind to everyone, not just those who have a roof over their heads. Miss Benedict is working as a housekeeper at the jail."

Clara snickered. "I'll bet."

Noah's quick intake of breath was the only indication he was angry. Rosalyn, however, had had enough.

"Listen here, you've no call to be mean to me or call me names. I ain't never done anything to you. The sheriff hired me to *clean*, not share his bed, not that you would even know what sharing a bed means, fattie."

Clara's face grew florid. "You little whore—"

"That's enough." Noah's command cut through the heated air. "There's to be no more insulting each other. We came here as customers, Miss Cartman. I'm sure at some point you will be in need of my services and I'd hate to think an upstanding citizen like you wouldn't receive them."

Noah's threat made Clara step back a pace. "You saying you wouldn't help me if I needed it?"

"I'm saying that charity begins at home. This town is my home now as much as it's yours and Miss Benedict's. We need to treat everyone with respect or there won't be any peace." He gestured to the curtain behind Clara. "Now if you wouldn't mind, Miss Benedict is in need of a bath and you have the nicest bathing house in town."

Rosalyn was about to point out there were only two in town and one was for men only, mostly cowboys, when Noah pushed her toward the dark blue curtain.

Clara's eyes narrowed. "You vouching for this piece of trash?"

"I specifically asked for no more name calling, Miss Cartman. With my help, Marina can make sure no one uses your facility anymore."

Now that was a direct threat. Rosalyn wanted to clap, but figured a smirk would do. Unfortunately, Clara's gaze was locked on Noah so she didn't see it.

"You'd do that?"

"I would. You can't treat people like offal, Miss Cartman. What we do to others comes back to us tenfold." He started walking Rosalyn back toward the curtain again. "With your permission?"

Clara flapped her hand. "Fine then, go ahead."

With a polite nod, Noah ushered Rosalyn into the bathing room and to her first hot bath in more than ten years. There were six bathtubs, positioned a couple of feet apart. She stepped up to the closest one and stuck her finger in the water.

"It's cold." She backed away. "I told you I wasn't taking a cold bath."

Noah touched her back to stop her retreat, the heat from his hands seeping through the dress and into her skin. The man had big hands, ones that made her wonder what they'd feel like on other parts of her body.

"Don't worry, Rosalyn. They keep the water hot in the back. They keep the tubs half full until someone comes in to use them."

"That'll be four bits." Clara stood behind them, arms folded across her chest.

Noah dug around in his pocket, pulled out money, then handed it to Clara. "She gets fifteen minutes."

"Ten minutes, no more than that."

"Fifteen. She's got long hair, it'll take five just to rinse it." Noah took a hank of her hair in his hand and lifted it up.

Rosalyn shuddered at the sensation and had to stop herself from running out the door. The sheriff needed to keep his hands to himself or she'd never survive this job.

When he let her hair go, she did step away, finally able to take a breath. Two boys came in with buckets of steaming water and poured them into the tub in front of her. Wisps of steam rose from the tub.

Noah stuck his fingers in the water. "It feels pretty warm now."

His gaze locked with hers and Rosalyn felt herself falling into the brown depths of his eyes. The warmth of the room became very, very hot. What was happening to her?

"I, uh, brought you some soap and a cloth." Noah handed her a bundle and skedaddled like a wisp of smoke, and she was left alone in the bathing room.

She unwrapped the cloth and found some pretty purple soap and a comb inside. Putting the bar under her nose, she inhaled and closed her eyes. It smelled like a meadow of flowers. She couldn't wait to use it.

Rosalyn shimmied off her new dress and laid it on the chair near the door. She didn't want to get it dirty in this place.

Glancing down at her tattered chemise, Rosalyn contemplated leaving it on to wash it in the water. It wouldn't hurt anything, besides she'd feel safer with it on, especially if Clara decided to stomp back in.

The moment her toes touched the warm water, a shiver slid up her body. Oh, hell, she'd had no idea hot water felt so good. Either that or she'd blocked out the memory for self-preservation.

She slid into the water as slowly as she could, savoring each inch of the bliss. By the time she'd settled deep into the tub, she couldn't wipe the grin off her face. Heaven. Absolute heaven.

After ducking her head to wet her hair, she lathered up and washed from head to foot, then did it again. She devoted special care to her hair. Years ago, she'd lost the brush she carried and did her best to finger-comb her thick locks. It hadn't done much good and as a result her hair was like a tangled bramble bush.

She rinsed it a second time until it squeaked beneath her fingers. After washing herself, she scrubbed her chemise until it didn't look quite as gray. Rosalyn didn't know how much time had passed but she wasn't about to get out of the tub until the last second. She closed her eyes and floated in the warm water.

Noah stepped outside and took a deep gulp of air. He had started shaking when he walked into the bathing room with Rosalyn. The heat, the steam and his surprisingly overpowering lust for her almost did him in. Rosalyn seemed to have some kind of special magic within her, one that reached out to him at an elemental level. It wasn't just unexpected, it was somewhat frightening.

He spent time simply watching the folks walking by at the end of their day, observing everyone and everything. For all appearances, it was a typical town. However, he saw the way ladies kept their eyes down and men barely nodded a greeting to each other. Something was wrong, he just didn't know what. Yet.

His father had taught him a great deal about how to study and process what he saw. His instincts were all screaming at him now. Chancetown wasn't the happy place he'd first thought it was. Appearances aside, it was his job to find out what or who was the bad apple in this barrel. He'd start with discovering what he could about the ranchers' feud and work his way back to Mayor Dickinson.

"Done."

The smell of lavender soap washed over him and he turned to find Rosalyn at his elbow. Freshly scrubbed, with pink cheeks and wavy, clean black hair, she snatched his breath away. The smile on her face faded as Noah stood there absorbing the sight of how incredible, how stunning she looked without the grime she'd hid behind.

"My God."

She frowned and turned to walk away. "I know I ain't beautiful, but you don't need to—"

He grasped hold of her elbow. "That's not it. Please, wait."

"Let go of me," she growled.

"You're exquisite."

She stopped pulling and turned back to look at him. "What does that word mean?"

"It means that you're the most beautiful thing I've ever seen." He swallowed the rest of what he wanted to say, that she was perfect, amazing and the most fascinating woman he'd ever met. Noah kept those thoughts to himself—he didn't want to scare her.

"Really? Are you just saying that to get in my britches?" She narrowed her gaze.

"First of all, you're not wearing britches and second of all, no, I'm not. I don't know what I have to do to prove that to you." He held out his arm. "May I walk you back to the jail?"

Noah had the sinking feeling that he'd made a huge mistake. As far as he could tell, the townsfolk had ignored Rosalyn for years. Now she'd be lucky if anyone didn't notice her. They would know just how amazing she was, and no doubt she'd be a target for every cowboy in town, not to mention strangers who were just passing through. Cleaning her up had revealed a diamond in the rough who he was now even more responsible for.

If his mother were here, he'd ask her for advice. However, his mother was hundreds of miles away and Noah was old enough to puzzle out his own problems. He had to figure out what to do with Rosalyn now that she was most assuredly in need of his protection.

As they walked back to the jail, he was assaulted by the clean scent of her again. Lord, he'd never make it alone with her if just the smell of soap made him hard. He knew it wasn't simply the soap, but Rosalyn herself who sent his blood pumping.

When they arrived back at the jail, Rosalyn stopped outside the door. Noah glanced at her, noting the set of the stubborn little chin.

"I cain't sleep in there again tonight."

"Why not?"

She waved her hand in the air. "I didn't sleep good the last two nights 'cause I don't trust you, Noah Calhoun. I ain't trusting nobody that easily even if you did pay for that nice bath." Her violet eyes flashed. "A man is a man, no matter what clothes he wears. Your eyes are hungry."

Noah swallowed the protest that rose to his lips. "If you change your mind, I can leave the door open for you."

Rosalyn frowned. "I ain't changing my mind. You make me jumpy and that means I cain't trust you."

Keeping his voice light, Noah opened the door. "I know what it means to not trust anyone." He noticed a wet piece of cloth clutched in one hand but didn't want to mention her unmentionables. It wasn't unusual to wash underthings while taking a bath.

Of course that brought home the realization that she was naked under the dress. His trousers grew impossibly tight and he had to make an escape before he embarrassed himself.

"I hope you come back tomorrow." Noah met her gaze. "Take care of yourself, Rosalyn. The door is always open for you."

As he stepped over the threshold, he had to hold himself back from grabbing her and dragging her inside. She'd survived for ten years without his help, one night wouldn't make a difference.

If he had any say in the matter, it would be the last night.

Rosalyn watched him disappear into the jail and wondered why the heck she wanted to follow him. She'd just met the man, and had fought with him on more than one occasion. He was a stranger, a man, someone not to trust. Yet she'd spent two nights beneath his roof locked in a cell holding the only key. If someone asked her why, she couldn't explain it. But now, things were different.

He'd changed her by making her take a bath. Rosalyn was smart enough to recognize the look in his eyes, the one that made her stomach flip. It had become too dangerous for her to stay.

She clutched the wet chemise in one hand, the steady drops of water puddling near her shoes. Rosalyn hadn't trusted many people in her life. In fact, she hadn't trusted anyone. Noah threatened the walls she'd built around herself.

Whirling around, she headed down the alley and back to her safe place. She needed to think about what had happened before she did something stupid.

The night sky was just a sliver above her, and Rosalyn counted the stars she could see. They sparkled against the velvet blackness, inviting her mind to imagine who was up there watching over her.

She hoped it was her mama, even if folks said she had sinned in the eyes of God. Rosalyn believed if there was a heaven, her mama was there, keeping watch. Sometimes she must've looked away though, like that awful time about five years ago when that handsome stranger had caught Rosalyn alone in the alley behind the hotel. She'd been charmed by his pretty words, then he'd shown his true colors when he'd forced himself on her. A shudder wracked her body at the memory, the despair and pain that had raged through her.

Rosalyn had railed at the heavens, wondering why she'd been left on Earth all alone. From then on, she'd been able to use her wits and skills to avoid most trouble.

Until Noah Calhoun entered her life.

He was trouble with a capital T.

"Mama, why did you let him catch me?" she whispered. "I ain't done nothing wrong, except for pushing him in the water. He is nice though and pretty to look at for sure."

She absently petted Whiskers, soothed by the sound of the cat's purr against her side.

"I ain't met nobody like him before. He makes me feel funny inside and that scares me." She pointed at the brightest star in the sky. "If that's you up yonder, I could use your help, Mama."

As if answering, the star twinkled and winked. Rosalyn smiled and shook her head.

"Whatever it is you're planning up there with God, I surely hope it's good."

Chapter Five

Rosalyn dreamed of Noah, as if her mind couldn't stop thinking about him even when she was asleep. She woke up with grainy eyes and an irritable disposition, dang that sheriff.

Whiskers appeared to sense her mood, because she ran off just as soon as Rosalyn awoke. Cats were smart creatures for sure.

When Rosalyn emerged from the alley behind Marina's, the high position of the sun told her she was late. It had to be after nine o'clock, well past the breakfast hour at the two restaurants in town. The slop buckets would be cold and congealed, if not empty. With a grumpy sigh, she accepted a hungry belly would be her companion for the next couple of hours.

Normally Rosalyn would eat breakfast, then go for a walk down to the creek just outside town, sometimes take a nap, other times wander behind buildings looking for treasures. Today she didn't want to do any of those things. She wanted to see Noah.

"Dang it!" Rosalyn stomped her foot, earning a few leery gazes from folks on the sidewalk. "That man has got to get out of my head."

She headed to the jail and the sheriff, determined to push him out of her mind and heart so she could get sleep and food on a regular basis. No telling what would happen if she continued on like this. It had to stop.

Noah had dreamed of Rosalyn. Some erotic, some sweet, others filled with images of what could happen to her. He tossed and turned most of the night, snatching sleep in small increments. When he dragged himself out of bed near dawn, his eyes were grainy and his disposition worse.

Elsa steered clear of him at the restaurant. She simply brought him breakfast after a cursory greeting, then let him be. No doubt the entire town was talking about how he'd brought Rosalyn to the bathing house. That more than anything bothered him. She didn't deserve to be gossiped about, but he knew it was happening. He'd even received a few sidelong glances and smirks.

The last thing he wanted to do was hurt her, yet the town seemed determined to make that happen. He needed to think of a way to keep her safe without damaging her reputation any more than he already had. When leaving Elsa's, he carried some ham biscuits and peaches with him. He didn't know if Rosalyn would appear for breakfast or not, however his conscience could not let him leave without food for her.

As he stepped outside the restaurant, he looked down the alley next to Elsa's, remembering his first encounter with Rosalyn. A smile crept across his lips at the memory of chasing her. It hadn't seemed funny at the time, but really, it was. She'd kept him running in circles ever since.

He tipped his hat to folks as he walked back to the jail, his mind definitely not concentrating on the faces passing him. When he opened the door, he half expected her to be sitting on the floor sorting the papers again. Or maybe he hoped that's where she'd be.

Either way, he was disappointed because she wasn't there. The echoing loneliness of the small building reminded him that Rosalyn had no obligation to him. He set the basket with the biscuits and peaches on the desk and sat down.

The next few hours passed by in a blur. Several folks stopped by for help with a missing pig, a garden-eating goat and a stolen crate of pickles. Surprisingly, he found himself enjoying the job. He helped find the pig, corral the goat and catch the pickle thief. It made him forget about Rosalyn for a while, sort of.

After a stern lecture to the boy who'd taken the pickles, Noah returned to the jail. The scent of lavender, of Rosalyn, washed over him, and his heart kicked his ribs.

"Rosalyn?"

She poked her head up from behind the desk, a cobweb stuck to one curl on the side of her head. "Whoever cleaned this place was an idiot."

Noah smiled, his day that much better with her there. She filled in the hole he'd felt in his chest all day.

"Why do you say that?"

She harrumphed. "They swept all the dirt under the desk and the cots in the cells." Rosalyn straightened, dust peppering the blue of her dress. She stretched, pressing the fabric against the curves of her ample breasts.

Noah's smile faltered as his body reacted to the sight. "I should tell the mayor to get a refund from Cherry and Bitsy then."

"Oh, that's who cleaned? No wonder it's dirty." She wrinkled her nose. Noah fought the urge to kiss her. "I dropped a piece of paper and got stuck in their mess."

"Have you eaten breakfast?" he blurted, trying to focus on something other than kissing her. He didn't need to think about her in that way. She was under his protection, not his lips.

She frowned. "No, why, did my stomach howl?"

This time his smile was so wide, it hurt his cheeks. "I brought you some breakfast a couple of hours ago. It's probably cold by now but—"

Rosalyn laughed, her eyes crinkling at the corners. "Cold food don't bother me."

Noah almost blushed. He'd plumb forgotten she'd lived on the streets for ten years.

"It's ham biscuits and peaches." He gestured to the basket covered with the napkin on the desk. "I thought you might be hungry."

Her violet eyes darkened and she looked away. "That was right nice of you, Sheriff."

"Please." He swallowed. "Call me Noah."

"Noah." Her voice sounded husky, different somehow.

The air between them felt heavy, making the small hairs on his neck stand at attention. His blood ran through him in a crazy rhythm, as time seemed almost to stop. The only two people in the world stared at each other. She licked her lips and his body jerked as if she'd scalded him.

"What are you doing to me?" she whispered.

"The same thing you're doing to me." He stepped toward her and she stepped back.

"I ain't ready to be your bed partner." Rosalyn held up her hands to stop him.

"I didn't, that is, I don't... Ah hell, I don't know what I'm doing." Noah ran a hand through his hair. "I'm a bit lost here."

"That makes two of us." She swallowed and glanced at the plate. "Maybe I should just take the vittles and go."

Noah wanted to protest, to tell her to stay, but he didn't. He truly didn't want her to feel obligated to him, even if his head, heart and body battled over exactly what he did want.

"You do whatever you need to, Rosalyn." Noah stood still as she wrapped the biscuits in the napkin and started toward the door.

Rosalyn turned and pierced him with her gaze. "One of these days I'm gonna figure out what's going on, but for now I say thanks. I, uh, might be back later for supper, if'n you want to eat with me again."

Noah grinned. "I'll be here waiting for you."

She nodded and disappeared out the door, taking Noah's concentration with her.

It was going to be a long afternoon.

ℬ

"You need to get those wooly bastards offa my property. They're eating all the grass and my cattle are going to starve this summer." Shep Seeger leaned over the desk and stuck his face into Noah's. "Do something."

Noah controlled the urge to lean back. The rancher had a corncob up his ass about his neighbor, and Noah was the recipient of the temper tantrum. Shep had the look of a man who'd been on a horse most of his life—bow-legged, leathery skin and calluses born of hard work. Unfortunately he also had the arrogance of a man used to getting his way. That rubbed Noah so much he had a hard time keeping his temper in check.

"What do you want me to do, Mr. Seeger?" Noah stood, straightening his vest. "I'd like to settle this friendly-like without bloodshed."

"Ain't no being friendly with that man Finley. That bastard is trying to use those fucking sheep to drive me off. I won't have it." He slammed his meaty fist onto the desk. "You get rid of him or I will."

"I'm sure we can come to an agreement. Let me talk to Mr. Finley. Maybe it was just a misunderstanding." He had no idea who the man was or how to find him, but he needed to calm Seeger down.

"Misunderstanding?" Seeger snorted. "I don't think so. I tried to help that sheepherder when he came into town, but no more. He's taking food out of my young'uns' mouths now." The man's face flushed an even deeper red.

Noah understood the need to protect your children and some of Seeger's anger made sense. Not all of it though. He had a gut feeling that some of it was for show.

"You said Finley didn't speak English well, right? Well, that could explain it." Noah wasn't fool enough to believe it, but acting like a smiling idiot who did might be the best tactic.

"Sounds like a shovelful of shit to me." Seeger's bushy eyebrows formed a single angry line.

"I promise you, Mr. Seeger, I will get to the bottom of the problem and find a resolution for both of you."

"You do that." Seeger's finger felt like a granite stick as he poked Noah in the chest. "Just get him off my land or I swear to God I'll kill every one of those fucking wooly bastards."

Seeger walked toward the door, then stopped and turned back. "What are you doing with that girl?"

Noah had hoped the town hadn't yet noticed Rosalyn or that he had spent time with her. A false hope obviously.

"I'm helping her." Noah tried to sound nonchalant, not defensive, his first instinct.

"There's lots more folks in this town who need help from the sheriff other than that ragamuffin. Like ranchers who pay your salary."

Noah wondered what Seeger meant about paying the sheriff's salary. Noah knew he had to step lightly or risk alienating a powerful man. The last thing he wanted to do was end an investigation before it even began. "Every citizen of this town deserves my help, including Miss Benedict. I will be investigating your claims, Mr. Seeger."

"Damn right you will." With one last glare, the rancher walked out with his bow-legged gait and spurs jingling in the air. A shadow appeared beside Seeger. Just outside the door stood the two men Noah had chased out of Marina's saloon. Seeger nodded to them, holding up one finger as if to say he was almost done. It somehow didn't surprise him that the cattle rancher kept company with two men who had nothing better to do than bother saloon girls. That meant Seeger employed the worst kinds of hired hands, which was not a good sign.

Seemed like his first week on the job wasn't going to be uneventful. Noah kept reminding himself to be impartial, but Seeger's threats rankled him. He expected Boyton hadn't been very good at enforcing the law when he was sheriff. Perhaps he'd even bent it or ignored it when the need arose. Noah hated to make assumptions about people but so far he wasn't impressed with the men in the town.

While Seeger's complaint brewed, Noah again tried to sort through the papers the older sheriff had left behind. He didn't have much luck, and eventually gave up, giving his mind free rein to wander.

An hour later the door to the jail slammed open and another man walked in. He was big with wavy blond hair, bearing a strong resemblance to a Viking, and had a jaw he could cut rocks on. The man's footsteps echoed like thunder.

"You da sheriff?" Even his voice was deeper than an average man.

"Yes, sir, I am. Do you need help?" Noah reminded himself that as an officer of the law, he was not to be intimidated by every man who walked in.

"My name is Finley. You need to get that ijut Seeger off my land and make him stop killin' da sheep."

Oh Lord. Here was the other half of that battle. Why was he not surprised they both put in an appearance? Perhaps they planned on using the sheriff to fight their personal battle. "You're the sheep rancher?"

"Ya. That's me. You have something against sheep?" He stepped closer and the floorboards creaked.

"No, sir, I don't. I'm just trying to gather information." Noah picked up the pencil and paper from the desk beside him. "Tell me everything that happened."

After ten minutes his hand cramped from writing, yet Finley kept talking. Noah realized the man was repeating the same information and threw up his hand to stop him.

"Okay, I think I've got it, Mr. Finley. I will do my best to make peace between you and Mr. Seeger. For now, just stay on your property and try not to shoot anybody."

Finley left with as much bluster as his cattle-ranching neighbor. The windows shook when he slammed the door. Noah sat down hard in the chair and stared at his notes. Before he forgot all of it, he added the information that Seeger had given him, which wasn't enough. His first mistake on the job—not getting all the information. He'd have to ride out to Seeger's ranch and talk to him again.

ℰↃ

Rosalyn spent the day doing what she normally did, but her mind kept wandering back to him. To the sheriff. To Noah. For a moment there in the jail, she thought he might kiss her. The thought didn't bother her, in fact, it sent tingles racing through her.

She wanted to kiss him. Odd, the thought about kissing a man had never occurred to her before. She'd shied away from most folks, especially the male kind, and they left her alone for the most part. Now she was annoyed with herself for thinking about him all the damn time.

What was it about him? He was handsome for sure with brown hair and eyes, but she'd seen prettier men before. He was big, but she'd seen bigger. He was an average man with nothing special about him.

Yet she knew that wasn't true. There was something very special about him. He made her forget about everything but him. Well, he didn't make her do it, but just the very thought of him kissing her made her loco.

Rosalyn was used to doing for herself, making her own decisions and following through with them. That was what she needed to do now.

She had to kiss him.

Noah had been daydreaming about Rosalyn when the door flung open for the third time that day. His heart jumped into a gallop at the sight of the object of his dreams framed in the doorway. She kicked the door closed then, without a word, stormed over to his desk and grabbed hold of his shirt. She yanked him to his feet, and with a frustrated growl threw her arms around him and planted her lips against his. Noah flattened his palms behind him, lest he yank her even closer. As it was, her full breasts pushed against his chest and her pelvis cradled his growing erection as if it had been made to.

She was inexperienced at kissing, but she was a quick learner. Her fierce kisses led to softer ones that made him forget what day it was. After an extra minute of delicious heaven he wouldn't trade for anything, he finally pushed her away. His breath gusted out and he realized he'd been holding it. She'd turned him into a blubbering idiot.

"Why did you do that?" His voice came out ragged and hoarse.

Her reddened lips matched the pink flags on her cheeks. He didn't know if it was embarrassment or arousal. Noah figured it was a little of both.

"I just wanted to kiss you, I guess. Just to see what all the fuss was about. Ain't nobody ever kissed me before." She put two trembling fingers to her lips. "I guess it was okay."

Noah trembled too, with desire and confusion. "It was more than okay, but we can't do that anymore. If you want folks to respect you, then you need to act respectable."

"Respectable folks don't kiss?" She snorted.

"They kiss their wives and husbands, not the sheriff." He smiled through his need to grab her and kiss her until neither one of them could breathe.

"Sounds stupid to me."

Noah shrugged. "I guess. Now I have a few things to do. Will you stay here and keep sorting the papers?"

Rosalyn folded her arms across her chest. "You running away?"

"A little bit, but I do need to go. I'll be back by supper and we can eat together, okay?" Eating with Rosalyn had been such a relaxing, natural thing to do, he found himself looking forward to doing it again and again.

"Why can't I come with you?"

He hadn't expected that. "Do you know how to ride a horse?"

She fiddled with the small scrap of lace on the cuff of her dress. "No, but I'm a fast learner."

"Not that fast. If you really want to learn, I'll teach you, but not today." He rubbed his thumb on her cheek. "Can I count on you to stay here or will you be gone when I get back?"

Rosalyn scowled, then nodded. "I'll fix up the papers some more."

"Thank you." He kissed her on the forehead, cursing his own impulse, but unable to stop himself. Rosalyn was already in his blood, and he had a feeling it was too late to get her out.

Rosalyn was disappointed it hadn't gone any further than kissing, at least she thought she was. After the initial few moments kissing him, she realized it wasn't bad at all. In fact, it was downright amazing. His lips were soft but firm and the man could kiss like an angel.

She'd been telling the truth when she'd told him nobody had kissed her before. They'd done worse things, but never kissing, leastwise not on the mouth. Now she knew what all the fuss was about and she found herself wanting more of it.

Too bad he'd be gone the rest of the afternoon. With a sigh, Rosalyn went to work on the papers. She had no idea how much time had passed when the door opened. Fortunately she'd taken Noah's advice and was sitting at the desk instead of on the floor. The pretty blue dress was too nice to get all dirty.

Marina, the dark-haired lady from the saloon, walked in. She'd always been kind to Rosalyn, unlike lots of other folks in town. The surprise on the older woman's face told Rosalyn that the sheriff had not shared the news of his new deputy with Marina.

"Rosalyn. I didn't expect to find you here and you're...clean." Her cheeks colored. "I mean, you look pretty today."

Rosalyn laughed. "You can say it. I ain't been clean in a while, but the sheriff paid for a bath down at Clara's."

Marina's eyebrows went up. "Clara let you in?"

"Not quite. The sheriff made sure she let me in." Rosalyn shrugged. "He said a deputy needed to be clean."

"A deputy?" Marina finally closed the door behind her. "What do you mean, a deputy?"

Rosalyn tried not to get angry, but it was hard. "You don't think I'm good enough?"

"No, that's not what I said." She stepped toward the desk, her eyes full of concern. "Mayor Dickinson isn't going to like a woman deputy, no matter who she is."

Rosalyn hadn't considered that before. Most folks paid her no mind, no matter what she was doing, although some kicked her around a bit. It was hard to believe that the mayor, a man she didn't know, could make a decision about her life.

"Is Dickinson the fat bald man who eats double portions at Elsa's?"

Marina chuckled. "Yep, that's him. He considers this town to be his personal property, and that includes the people who live here."

"That's crazy talk. I don't belong to no one." Rosalyn's heart fluttered at the possibility that someone would make her leave the jail, and Noah. "He can't make me leave."

Marina sat on the chair next to the desk, the old wood creaking. "I'm afraid he can, or Noah could lose his job. It's true that Sheriff Boyton had permission to pick his replacement, but the town pays Noah's salary. He has to do what the mayor tells him to."

That was not good news. It made her stomach flip and bile rise up her throat. She'd just found a place where she felt safe and a man she was beginning to trust. Rosalyn didn't want to leave, a fact that surprised her a bit. She hadn't depended on anyone for a long time and wasn't ready to start.

"What should I do?" In this area, Rosalyn was at a loss. She didn't want Noah to lose his job because of her.

"For starters, I wouldn't go around telling people you're a deputy. Are you staying here with him, alone?"

Rosalyn's guard slammed up again. "Not really. I slept in the cell a couple times but I had the keys. Noah slept upstairs. We ain't doing no bed sport."

"I believe you, but others might not. Just be careful." Marina laid a hand on Rosalyn's, the heat from her slender fingers contrasting with the icy chill that had taken hold of Rosalyn. "If you ever need help, please know that you can come to me. In fact, you can live at the saloon if you'd like. I have a spare room next to mine."

It was tempting. Staying with Marina would keep Noah out of trouble with the town and that fat mayor. In the few days she'd known Noah, there hadn't been one moment they spent together that she didn't remember.

"Thanks, but I'm going to stay here for now." Rosalyn refused to lower her gaze or be ashamed of the fact that she chose to stay.

Marina squeezed her hand. "I understand. He's wonderful, isn't he? If I were fifteen years younger, I'd probably fall in love with him, too."

Rosalyn started to protest that she wasn't in love with him, but the words caught in her throat. He was the first man to be kind to her, to show her respect and treat her as a lady instead of a nuisance. He *was* wonderful and she wanted to hold onto that wonderful for just a bit longer.

ၰ

Noah was going to ride out to Seeger's ranch first, but decided to visit Finley instead. Something about Seeger struck Noah as wrong, and he didn't appreciate the fact that the rancher had threatened him the first time they met. He'd bet everything he had, which was basically what he was riding, that Seeger was the source of the problem, not the sheep-herding Finley. The rivalry between cattlemen and sheepherders had become a big problem in the middle of cattle country where sheep were considered a plague.

The warm spring breeze lifted his spirits, as did the memory of Rosalyn's kiss. He'd probably remember that for the rest of his life. It wasn't as if Noah hadn't been kissed before, or been with a woman. Uncle Trevor had made sure of that. The way Rosalyn approached life, and the absolute honesty in how she dealt with everything struck a chord, as did the haunted look that lurked deep in her violet eyes.

After an hour of mooning over the woman he'd made into a deputy, Noah heard and smelled sheep. He rode up on a rise and found a bowl-shaped valley with a herd of the wooly beasts milling around on the green grass. Three dogs circled the herd, keeping their charges in check with a bark now and then. He didn't see any people.

A rifle cocked behind him. "You have good reason to be on my land, ya?"

"Mr. Finley, it's Sheriff Calhoun." He didn't want to alarm the man so he didn't reach for his pistol, which had been his first instinct.

"Sheriff? You come see me, then?"

After a rustling in the trees behind him, Finley rode out on an enormous gray horse that had to be eighteen hands high. The blond giant kept his pistol up and ready.

"Yes, I came to see you because you filed a complaint against Mr. Seeger. I'm here to investigate your problems." He hoped like hell it would be a simple misunderstanding, but life was never simple.

"Ya, good. You come down and see what happen this week." Finley released the hammer on the rifle and slipped it back into the holster on the saddle.

Noah rode behind the rancher, scanning the valley for any movement. He'd let his guard down because he'd been obsessing over Rosalyn. Noah knew he couldn't afford to let that happen anymore. Finley was a simple sheepman, but no doubt there were other, less respectable men out there. Maybe even watching them now.

His gut instinct was telling him they were definitely being tracked and watched. Someone was very interested in what the sheriff did or didn't do with Finley. He'd step lightly, waiting and watching to see who or what he could.

"How long have you lived here, Mr. Finley?" Might as well start at the beginning and work his way forward. Noah had a feeling this was not a new problem.

"A year last February. Mr. Seeger, he never liked my sheep, but they are good creatures that bring many good things to folks. Those cattlemen couldn't keep warm without my wool for their sweaters and socks." Finley's pride in his sheep was evident in his voice.

They reached the bottom of the hill and slowed the horses so as not to startle the sheep. The smell of sheep grew stronger, and Noah wondered how long it took to get used to it. Probably not too long, as he got used to the smell of cattle from a young age.

"When did you start having problems?"

"Six months later, right after I sell my wool for the fall. Seeger come around and threaten me and says my sheep eat too much grass." Finley waved his arm. "They stay on my ranch, not on open range, but he don't give up. He complain to the old sheriff. That's when I find out that Seeger have trouble selling his cows because they're too thin."

A significant reason to go to war with someone, greed. Greed had destroyed many lives and would likely destroy more. It was the driving force behind countless awful things.

The bleat of the sheep grew louder and soon it was hard to hear Finley. The big man gestured to the left so Noah followed him to a small outcropping of rocks where they dismounted. The grass around it was chewed down, letting the imprints in the dirt be more visible. Noah squatted down and saw at least two different boot prints, neither of which matched Finley's enormous feet.

"Look between the rocks there. On the right." Finley pointed to an opening where the lichen had covered part of the rocks.

Noah peered in and the smell of rotting flesh assaulted him. He clapped a hand over his nose and looked closer. The bodies of at least half a dozen lambs were scattered in the foot high space. Dried rust-colored blood matted their fur.

"What happened to them?"

"I find them like this two days ago. Each one had their necks sliced open and thrown in there." Finley shook his head. "Poor little lambs were only a week old. I left them there for sheriff to see. Now that's you."

Noah knew the sheep rancher would never have killed six of his lambs himself. The future of any herd was in the young it produced. He swallowed the protest that he wasn't qualified to investigate a crime like this. That would have been a lie—he just had to find the courage and gumption to stand tall and uncover the truth, no matter who was guilty.

"Anything else to show me?" Noah's mind raced with the problems that arose from the bodies of the wooly babes.

Finley reached into his saddlebags and pulled out a cloth-wrapped bundle. When he opened it, Noah recognized the coyote traps immediately. His family had never used them because they were too cruel to any creature, but others had no qualms about using anything at their disposal. From what he could see, the steel wires were stained with blood.

"More lambs?"

"Ya, and a young ewe that didn't know any better. So far, there have been seventeen of my sheep killed. Another eighty-seven have disappeared. I think to someone's table for dinner." Finley clenched the wooden stakes of the trap until they cracked. He looked up at Noah with fury in his blue eyes. "You will help me, Sheriff? I have no one else."

Faced with the very real issue that was up to him to solve, Noah stepped off the safe path and into the black unknown of being a lawman. "Yes."

၈၃

It didn't take long for Noah to reach Shep's ranch—it bordered Finley from the north. The lowing of cows and the sharp tang of manure told him he was definitely in cattle territory. After his discussion with the sheepman, he was convinced that more than one person was involved in the attacks.

Several things had happened at once, which would indicate a multiple-pronged attack. Obviously whoever was behind it was intelligent and cunning. That made Noah's job harder and escalated the danger level even higher.

Shep had to have at least a thousand cattle in the valley, more than Noah had seen in quite some time. The Malloys and Calhouns had good herds, but this was beyond even that scope. No rancher kept his cattle in the same area—they were usually spread around in various pastures. Shep had deep pockets judging by the size of his herd, which meant he could hire anyone he needed to, if he wanted to.

One cowboy galloped toward Noah. Three others remained with the herd. As the man drew closer, Noah wasn't surprised that it was Shep Seeger.

"Sheriff," he said as he approached. "'Bout time you got your ass out here. Glad you finally made it." The sneer never left his face.

Noah took the sarcasm in stride. "There are a great deal of issues to deal with in Chancetown. I have to deal with the most pressing first."

"Like fucking that alley whore?" Seeger spit chaw at the tall grass beneath the horse.

Tired of being polite and eating this man's shit with a spoon, Noah's temper snapped. He reached across the horse and grabbed the other man by the throat, squeezing with just enough pressure to make Seeger's veins bulge.

"I might be new to this town, Seeger, but where I come from we respect our women."

"What the hell are you doing?" the rancher gasped out.

The roar of rage that echoed in Noah's heart gripped him so tightly he could barely pull in a breath. It wasn't about Seeger, but more about how people treated others.

"Apologize," Noah snarled.

Seeger's eyes promised retribution. "I'm sorry," he spat.

Noah released the pressure slowly, keeping his other hand on the butt of his pistol. "You keep a civil tongue from now on. I'm here to investigate your complaint, not listen to your filthy mouth."

As the red faded from his vision, Noah sat back on his saddle. "If you're ready to give me more information, I'm ready to listen." His hand shook as he pulled paper and pencil from his saddlebag, keeping his eyes on a furious-looking Seeger.

"Finley's been running his sheep on my property. I'll show you the damage he's caused." Seeger rubbed his throat and continued to glare at Noah. "If you're through trying to kill me, I'll bring you out there."

Noah didn't know what had gripped him, but as it faded, he realized he'd put himself in a precarious position by threatening

81

Seeger. Still he couldn't regret it. Seeger needed to know he couldn't threaten the law, even if he was a newborn sheriff.

"I'd be glad to. First give me the details." He held up the pencil.

"You're a bastard, you know that?" Seeger growled.

Noah showed his teeth, but he didn't smile. "Yes, so don't forget it."

ℰℴ

The sun had already set by the time Noah made it back to Chancetown. His head swam with everything he'd seen and been told. Exhaustion crept over him and the thought that Rosalyn might be waiting for him at the jail was the only bright spot in an otherwise tumultuous day.

When he arrived at the jail, he wasn't pleased to see Mayor Dickinson striding towards him. Noah dismounted with a sigh and waited. By the look on the other man's face, Noah wasn't going to like whatever the mayor had to say.

"Calhoun."

"Evenin', Mayor."

The mayor stepped in close, his pudgy face lined with perspiration. "I hear that you're not the only one living at the jail."

Noah knew he'd have to step lightly. He didn't want Rosalyn to be hurt, but he also wanted to make sure both of them didn't end up eating the scraps from Elsa's restaurant.

"Who told you that?"

The mayor pursed his lips. "It don't matter who told me. I'm asking you now. Is there someone else living at the jail with you?"

"No. I had a little bit of trouble with one of the townsfolk. She learned her lesson and was released. Exactly what I would have done with anyone who was disturbing the peace." Noah could lie with the best of them. He could tell people he didn't trust what they wanted to hear. When he tried the same tactic with people who knew him well, whom he cared about, it backfired.

"So you're telling me that girl who's been hiding in the alleys for years, that filthy bedraggled creature who probably has head lice, the clap and God knows what other kind of disease, is *not* living in that jail with you?" His eyes blazed with suspicion.

This time Noah didn't have to lie. "There is no filthy, bedraggled creature living at the jail." That, at least, was the truth.

The mayor tipped his brown bowler hat back and peered at Noah, who kept his face intentionally blank and bland.

"You're not lying to me, are you, Calhoun?"

"What would be the purpose of lying to you, Mr. Dickinson?"

"Well, I understand, son, that every man needs a little pussy now and then. Sheriffs are no exception. They have dicks just like every other man. How you use it is my business. You can go down there to the whorehouse and satisfy any itch you get, but I will not have you fucking that woman in my jail. Is that clear?" The toothy grin tucked away, the mayor was showing his true colors for the first time.

Noah's anger threatened. He was usually able to keep all of his emotions in check. Ever since he arrived in Chancetown, his life had been turned upside down and everything he thought he knew, he didn't. Somehow Rosalyn had opened a Pandora's box of emotions. He needed to figure out some way to rein them in.

Noah had to grip his temper with both hands and hang on tight. "I assure you, Mr. Dickinson, I've done no fucking in this jail." He stepped back and secured his horse to the hitching post. "Did you need anything else, sir?"

"You know, I know who your father is. Tyler Calhoun is a famous name in certain circles." Dickinson rocked back and forth on his heels.

The mention of Tyler made a bad situation worse. One thing Noah didn't want was to come up short while being compared to his famous bounty-hunter father.

"What a coincidence, I know him too."

"Don't you be smart with me, boy." The mayor waved a chunky finger in Noah's face. "You can be as much of a hardass as you want, but you still work for me. Your father was known for getting his man, dead or alive. I'm expecting the same from you. I know you were out at Finley's. You just remember how your father worked and get your man, dead or alive. We expect our sheriff to do what's best for the town, not what his britches tell him to do."

Noah flattened his lips into a tight white line, keeping the fury behind his teeth. After a minute of staring at each other, the mayor finally dropped his gaze. Noah felt a smidge of triumph.

"Since you're only working ten days of the month, you only get paid for those ten days. You'll get a full month's salary in June." The mayor carefully counted out Noah's pay and handed it to him. "I paid Cherry and Bitsy for cleaning the jail for you. I'm late for dinner with my wife. Just remember everything I said, Calhoun. Have a nice evening."

Noah stood there, breathing in deeply and letting the air out for a good five minutes before he was able to unclench his jaw. He shook with the force of his anger and disgust. It wasn't as if Noah hadn't been exposed to the underbelly of human existence before. He knew just how deep and dark that cave was—he'd been there. However, to find blatant prejudice, corruption and vicious greed in one tiny town surprised him. There was no question he'd be able to handle it. He'd survived worse so he wasn't worried about himself. He could pick up and move on.

Rosalyn was a different story.

Noah was worried about her. He'd already changed her by pulling her from the streets, by making her bathe and wear clean clothes. Those changes put her in a precarious position with the town. He had to follow through on his commitment to helping her. Noah wouldn't allow Rosalyn to suffer because of his actions. He slapped his hat on his leg and walked into the jail, still wondering how the hell he could save her and himself without getting killed in the process.

Chapter Six

Rosalyn had heard the two men talking out on the street, the filthy words that fat man said. She wanted to run out there to claw and kick him until he apologized. She knew Noah was protecting her and that he'd deliberately lied. That put him and his job at risk because of her, a situation she'd never wanted.

She didn't know quite what to do. No one had ever done that for her before. No one had stepped in front of her and protected her, at least not that she remembered. Maybe a long time ago when her parents were still alive, but a lot of her memories of that time were kind of blurry. She peeked out the window and saw Noah standing there, staring into nothing. His expression was hard as stone.

Rosalyn had the impulse to run out and put her arms around him, but even she knew that was a bad idea. The town seemed to be hell-bent on keeping the sheriff away from her. What she didn't know was why.

She waited in the shadows as the door opened and closed. Noah stepped in with a sigh. His face reflected many different emotions, including anger and frustration.

Without thinking about what she was doing, Rosalyn emerged from her hiding spot and rushed to him. Noah reached for his pistol, but before he could clear leather, she'd jumped on him. As her arms wound around his neck, her legs wrapped around his waist, pressing her pussy to him.

"What the hell?" Noah bumped into the door.

Rosalyn looked him in the eye. "Welcome back, Sheriff."

As her mouth descended on his, he tried to pull away, but she would have none of that. Rosalyn was going to seduce Noah. She was a bit inexperienced with her tongue, but a fast learner.

She licked her way from one side of his full lips to the other. Her nipples puckered against his hard chest, the tingles of awareness sliding down her skin straight between her legs. What had started as a reward for him was turning into something else altogether.

Her pulse beat a steady tattoo as his mouth opened and her tongue swept in. His mouth was a hot, wet cavern of delight, and she took advantage of every second of it. She tickled his teeth, his gums, his tongue and everything in between.

His cock hardened between her legs, pulsing and pushing against her cleft, raising her excitement level even higher.

"The cell, now," she forced out between kisses. As Rosalyn pulled at his hair, Noah obeyed her command, stumbling to the cell.

"Lay down." She slid off him, never losing contact with his mouth. With a grin, she pushed him onto the cot and unbuttoned his shirt. When his chest was finally hers to touch, she ran her fingers through the soft hairs that peppered the otherwise smooth skin. When her nails scratched at his flat nipples, he hissed against her lips.

"I think I found a good spot here." She smiled and waggled her eyebrows. Throwing one leg over him, she straddled him, effectively trapping the sheriff beneath her.

Noah's brown eyes were dilated with desire. He started to say something but Rosalyn put her hand over his mouth.

"Shut up and enjoy, cowboy."

Rosalyn kissed her way down his chest, pausing to suck and nibble at his dark pink nipples. He moaned, but otherwise his harsh breathing was the only other sound in the jail.

She knew anyone could walk in at any time, but it didn't matter. Her body screamed with ancient hunger, wanting to feed on that which Noah could give her—closeness, pleasure and a healthy dose of sex.

This time Rosalyn would be the one to tell him what to do, how to do it and when. She kissed her way down his belly, stopping to swirl her tongue in his bellybutton. The muscles tightened beneath her hands and mouth. The trail of dark brown hair led her down, down, down to the vulnerable part of him that called her.

She unbuttoned his trousers and gazed at the animal that lay trapped under his drawers. As it pulsed before her eyes, her body throbbed along with it. For the first time she could remember, Rosalyn's body responded to a man's with excitement. Her breasts and pussy ached with need. This was what the whores must like about fucking.

Rosalyn was determined to enjoy it.

She freed him from his drawers, gripping him in her fist. He groaned and tried to push her hands away.

"No you don't. I aim to taste this and you can't stop me."

As she got closer to his pulsing member, her bravado faltered but Rosalyn wasn't one to back down from anything. She licked the top of him, tasting salt and something that was pure Noah, the essence of who he was. A shiver raced over her skin and she knew everything would be all right.

"Stop, Rosalyn, stop. I can't... Please, stop." He closed his eyes, pushing against her, the veins standing out in his neck. "Don't do that."

Rosalyn could see by the look on his face that he meant it. He didn't want her to pleasure him with her mouth. The reasons weren't important—she recognized the truth in his eyes. That didn't mean she couldn't pleasure both of them in another way.

She pulled off her dress and climbed on top of him. As she positioned herself over him, he opened his eyes. Rosalyn impaled herself.

Oh, sweet saints above. He filled her completely, made her feel whole. Buried deep within her, he fit perfectly, as if he'd been made to be there. Like two sides of a coin, they were a matched set.

His hands tightened on her thighs. She rode him harder, sliding up and down on his engorged flesh. The sweet heat from their mingled breath and bodies warmed the cell until it felt like an inferno. The sound of flesh against flesh split the air.

"Oh God, Rosalyn," he barked as he pulsed deep within her.

Rosalyn rode the wave with him, the echoes of her pleasure mingling with his. Bliss settled over her, the first piece of peace and sweet harmony she'd experienced in a very long time, perhaps in all her life. She rocked back and forth until he started shaking. The metal feet vibrated against the wooden floor from the force of it. She opened her eyes and stared down at him in surprise.

A pair of tears made their way down his cheeks.

"Jesus Christ, Rosalyn. Why did you do that? I didn't want... God, I didn't want to turn this into something it wasn't."

He wiped his face. "I keep telling people you're not a whore and here we are having sex."

Rosalyn frowned. "I wanted to. That doesn't make me a whore."

"No, it doesn't, but that's not what other people will think." He squeezed the bridge of his nose. "I can't believe this just happened."

She climbed off, leaving him alone on the cot with their mingled essence on his skin. He started buttoning his pants, avoiding her gaze.

"You didn't like it then? Didn't seem that way to me." Hurt mixed with confusion made her sound angry.

"That's not what I meant." He stood and finished correcting his clothes.

Rosalyn noted his hands shook and fumbled with the buttons on his shirt. She looked up into his eyes and saw more than she expected—pain, pleasure, confusion—and didn't know what to do. Her experiences with men had been limited to Noah and one other and she hadn't even wanted to think about him.

"Don't worry about it, Sheriff. I was just scratching an itch." She forced a smile to her lips. "You were a good scratching post."

"Stop it." He took her by the shoulders. "Don't cheapen this. It was amazing and incredible." He swiped a hand down his face. "I don't even know what to say here. Rosalyn, we can't do this again."

An arrow of hurt slammed into her. "Fine, I won't. Now if you don't mind, I'm tired and need to get some sleep. I need to go." She hoped her shaking legs would carry her away. Rosalyn stepped toward him, grateful when he backed out of the cell so she didn't have to touch him. She wasn't sure she could've stopped herself from hitting him right about then.

Noah left the cell with a bow, then trudged up the stairs, his boot heels dragging. As the sound echoed through the jail, Rosalyn focused on breathing.

Rosalyn sat on the bed and wrapped her arms around her chest, trying to get her breath and her sense back. Giving Noah pleasure had seemed like a good idea, but obviously it wasn't. He said he shouldn't have done it. Maybe he was one of those men who liked other men. It didn't matter.

She wasn't about to touch him again.

Noah put his head between his knees and took deep breaths. The dizziness finally passed and he could sit up straight without needing to pass out.

Shit.

He'd known he was attracted to Rosalyn, but had it under control, or so he thought. Then she'd thrown herself at him and turned him into a blithering idiot with one swipe of her tongue.

His passions had been running high after the afternoon's intensity. He had lost himself in the feeling of Rosalyn, her scent, her touch, her black hair like a curtain blocking everything and everyone out. Her mouth had seemed inexperienced, that is until it closed around his dick.

He still throbbed and pulsed with the aftermath of the most intense orgasm of his life. Noah wasn't a ladies' man, but he'd had a woman seduce him before.

But not like that.

Not enough to make him lose his mind.

Noah took off his clothes and lay in bed confused, swirling with emotions he thought he had locked up tight. Rosalyn had turned him completely in circles. He'd never meant to have sex with her, certainly not on a jailhouse cot where anyone could have walked in on them. However he couldn't seem to stop himself. He might tell himself that he just went along with Rosalyn's seduction, but that was a bald-faced lie. His body buzzed, his mind tumbled thoughts around and he barely slept a wink.

When dawn arrived, Noah got up immediately, wanting and needing to talk to her. When he got downstairs, Rosalyn was gone.

The blue dress lay on the cot, folded in a neat square.

Rosalyn sat beneath the stairs behind Marina's saloon, willing herself not to grind her teeth anymore. Confusion and anger outweighed any hurt she'd felt at Noah's rejection. She hugged her knees to her chest and rocked back and forth, wishing Whiskers were there to give her furry comfort. She'd made a choice, a choice to see where a physical relationship with Noah would go. He was handsome, strong, kind— everything a woman could want in a man.

However, Rosalyn had wanted a temporary bed partner, not a life partner. The experience of seducing Noah had left her confused. The aftermath of what she thought had been a good idea had forced Rosalyn to run. Noah made it clear he didn't want to be with her because he was the sheriff. Rosalyn wasn't going to stay where she wasn't wanted. A man should only have to kick a dog once before it learns to protect itself.

She hadn't taken his gift though—she couldn't take anything from him. With any luck, he wouldn't find her. She couldn't risk staying with him any longer, and it wasn't as if she didn't warn him. She'd told him she would only stay as long as she wanted to. She wasn't beholden to him—he was just a stranger. So why did her heart ache?

For just a brief moment in time, Rosalyn had felt what everyday married folks do. A sense of belonging, of rightness, of knowing there was someone next to her she could touch and taste.

Now it was gone. She sighed and put her forehead on her knees.

The brown dress felt coarse against her skin. After having experienced the softness of the blue cotton dress, the brown fabric smelled and made her itch.

The difference between the dresses mirrored the ones between her and Noah. She might pretend for a while to live in his world, but in the end, Rosalyn had to return to the coarse brown dress and leave the soft, cotton world of Noah Calhoun behind. Chancetown wasn't enormous by any means, but it was big enough and Rosalyn knew it well. She could hide so he'd never find her. With any luck, he wouldn't try.

The smells of the alley weren't even the same. The rancidness of rotting food mixed with dirt, piss and shit all assaulted her nose. When had all of this changed? It had only been days, what was different now?

Rosalyn knew the answer. It wasn't the alley. It was her. Being with Noah had altered her. She only hoped she could reverse it or she might never survive. Living the way she did required wits and skills, not to mention good reflexes.

Rosalyn would just have to forget Noah. Of course, she might also try to stop the sun from rising or the moon from shining in the night sky.

ༀ

After a fruitless day of searching, Noah realized Rosalyn didn't want to be found. He got a few odd looks from townspeople, but nobody asked him what he was doing. By the time the sun had set, he was filthy, hungry and frustrated.

A solitary dinner brought home the realization that she was gone and likely intended to stay that way. The chicken that had looked so good sat like a rock in his stomach.

Two days later he swore he could still smell Rosalyn in the jail. If she hadn't left the dress behind, he might think that something bad had happened to her. The dress had been a message, a goodbye note. Noah hadn't found a trace of Rosalyn anywhere and he was growing worried. Unfortunately there wasn't a damn thing he could do about it.

Telling himself he wasn't going to search for Rosalyn again, Noah readied himself to walk the length of the main street when unexpected visitors arrived at the jail.

Mrs. Knudsen bustled in with a young lady who could only be her daughter. A smaller, younger version of the apple-cheeked blonde, the girl kept her gaze on the floor the first five minutes they were in the jail.

"Sheriff Calhoun," Mrs. Knudsen practically sang. "I've brought you some more strudel." She handed him a paper-wrapped package with a wide grin.

"Good morning, Mrs. Knudsen. That's very kind of you." He took the package, noting the weight of the strudel, which meant she'd used a precious supply to make it. Apples were not in season in May.

"It was no bother for our sheriff." She pushed the young woman forward. "This is my daughter Josephine. Say hello, Josephine."

"Hello." Barely audible, Josephine looked as though she wanted a hole to open up and swallow her.

Noah took pity on the girl. He'd been in that situation himself. "It's a pleasure to meet you, miss. Mrs. Knudsen, I was about to go make my afternoon rounds."

"Oh, but you have to stay for a few moments, ya? I wanted Josephine to have a chance to get to know you."

Noah tried to concentrate on Mrs. Knudsen and her quiet, demure daughter Josephine. In his mind's eye, he couldn't help but compare her to Rosalyn. Whereas Rosalyn was thin to the point of being gaunt, with jet black hair and the wild passion that couldn't be matched, Josephine was all soft gentility, with gentle curves and clean fingernails. Josephine was a nice girl, a perfect candidate if someone was looking for a wife. Noah was not that someone.

"So you will come to the dance in two weeks?" Mrs. Knudsen was saying. The hope in her face was a clear sign of exactly what she wanted from Noah.

He had a moment of panic when he tried to remember what she had said. "I'm not sure. I'll probably need to work that night, to keep the townsfolk safe for the dance."

It must've been the right thing to say because Mrs. Knudsen grinned. "That's good. We will see you there."

With a final nod, she ushered Josephine out the door. The younger woman threw him an apologetic glance before the two of them disappeared. Noah sighed. Things were getting complicated in Chancetown and he was right in the middle of it. Hopefully not standing in front of a preacher with a surprised look on his face.

Chapter Seven

The next week, Noah sent out telegrams to dig deeper into the ranchers' feud. There had to be something going on other than a sheep and cattle argument that had escalated to genuine violence. He contacted a few people in Houston and one in the county seat for information.

Until they got back to him, there was nothing to do but wait. The quiet man who ran the telegraph office and train station hadn't been nosy about what was in the telegram. However, that didn't mean he wouldn't share the information with Seeger. A powerful man like him had a lot of influence in a small town.

After he sent the telegrams, he felt a little bit more like the sheriff. Over the last two weeks, it had been a strange adjustment to go from aimless wanderer to responsible lawman. He'd tried too hard to be the old sheriff with a new pair of boots. Now, he needed to do the job as if he wasn't filling Sheriff Boyton's shoes, but rather adding his own pair.

While some folks still complained he didn't do things like Johnny, others now greeted him with a smile or a wave. He felt comfortable for the first time in many years. The next step was making the jail his own.

Noah spent hours organizing the sheriff's office and hanging the most recent wanted posters on the wall. At the bottom of the pile, Noah found one for Nicky Malloy. A jolt of homesickness hit him square between the eyes. His adopted mother had been close to his age when she'd gone on the run a dozen years ago, making the choice to leave home. He'd known that she'd had a bounty on her head, but finding it here seemed to be too much of a coincidence.

Obviously Sheriff Boyton had kept almost a library of wanted posters to have one at least ten years old. As Noah stared at the pencil sketch of his adopted mother, the ache of missing his family grew to enormous proportions. He hadn't contacted them in more than six months. With the ranchers' issues facing him in Chancetown, he could have used someone from his family to talk to, to sort it out in his head.

Noah talked to Elsa and Marina almost every day, but after having a brief taste of companionship with Rosalyn, he was lonely. He missed her. One of the things he liked about her was the fact that she spoke her mind, no matter what. No silly conversation just for the sake of it. Her forthrightness made her unique in a world of deception.

He folded the wanted poster and tucked it in his pocket. Some time ago, he'd lost the photograph of his family. This would have to suffice for a while.

∞

Rosalyn smelled fried chicken being cooked at Elsa's. The scent made her stomach howl louder than a coyote. She hoped the slops would include chicken legs. Lord how she loved those.

As she waited behind the crates, Rosalyn thought about the ache in her heart. It had been over a week since she'd seen Noah, or at least since he'd seen her. She'd spotted him a few days earlier behind the general store, peering beneath the back porch. As yet he hadn't discovered her spot under Marina's stairs, lucky for her. Since the building next door about blocked the view, it was the perfect hiding spot.

However, Rosalyn wasn't hiding. She was keeping to herself and staying out of the sheriff's way. It wasn't as if she needed him, but only that, well, she missed him.

Noah was a gentleman—a word Rosalyn hadn't known the meaning of until she'd met him. He'd treated her as a lady—if that wasn't laughable.

"What are you doing here, missy?"

Elsa's harsh words made Rosalyn jump a country mile. The diminutive restaurant owner stood over her, fists on hips and a frown on her face.

"Nothing. Just waiting for my cat." Rosalyn's voice trembled and she pinched her thigh to stop.

"Now I know you're fibbing. Come on out of there and come into the kitchen. I need to have a talk with you." Elsa turned and stomped up the three steps to the back door of the kitchen.

Rosalyn didn't know what to do, run from or to the woman. It seemed she didn't have much of a choice.

Elsa glared at Rosalyn. "Move it. I don't have but an hour before I have to start on supper."

With more than a few butterflies in her stomach, Rosalyn entered the kitchen of the restaurant. She hadn't been inside before, not that she could recall anyway. The smells from the bread, potatoes and meat surrounded her. She closed her eyes, reveling in the warm, homey air. Two large black cookstoves stood on the left side. A coffeepot and a kettle sat on one of them. A huge table sat in the middle, covered with all kinds of stuff, including pans, rolling pin, tins of flour and a bowl of eggs. On the right was a big sink with a faucet. Running water was something Rosalyn hadn't expected.

"Sit." Elsa pointed at the chair beside the stoves.

Rosalyn settled on the wooden seat, content to be in such a sweet-smelling place.

Elsa thrust a glass of milk at her. "You look like a stiff wind would blow you away, girl. Drink."

On a normal day Rosalyn wouldn't even be in the kitchen, much less drinking milk with the intimidating Elsa. Yet there she was, meekly taking the glass.

"What are you doing? I thought you were with the sheriff." Elsa went back to the table and rolled out biscuit dough.

Rosalyn swallowed the milk before she could choke on it. "What do you mean?"

Elsa waved a floury hand in the air. "I see things. I know things. You were there with him and he smiled every day. Now he frowns and scowls." She leveled an accusatory glare at Rosalyn. "Noah Calhoun is a good man. Don't let your pride get in the way."

Her mouth dropped open. "My pride? He didn't want me."

"Pshaw. I don't believe that for a second. The darkness in his eyes had lightened after he found you. Now the shadows are back." Elsa picked up a glass and cut out the biscuits with it. "Go see him."

Rosalyn's heart warred with her head. Was it true? Had Noah changed after meeting her? It hadn't occurred to her that he'd be affected by her. Elsa was right—Noah was a good man, the best. Someone had raised him right. He deserved better than a damaged woman like Rosalyn.

"Don't even start telling me that you're not worthy of him." Elsa seemed to be able to read Rosalyn's thoughts. "I knew your mama. She did all right by you until she died. She was a good person no matter what folks say about her. I don't think she could have raised a bad child."

Rosalyn's head spun with memories she'd blocked for so long. The men holding her back as the rope went around Mama's neck, the screaming, the crowd cheering. She dropped the glass and clapped her hands over her ears to block the sounds.

Small, firm hands pulled her wrists away. "You didn't have to break my glass, Rosie."

Rosie.

It was a fist to her gut. Her mother had called her that. It was one of those memories she'd buried beneath mounds of loneliness that had become her life.

She stared down at the broken glass glittering amidst the frothy white milk and wanted to vomit. Elsa put a hand on the back of her neck and pushed her forward.

"Put your head a'tween your knees before you add your breakfast to that mess." She rubbed Rosalyn's back.

After a few minutes the panic subsided and Rosalyn was able to take a deep breath. It had been quite a long time since she'd even thought about her mother or the way she'd died. Folks in town had never forgiven Marilyn Benedict for murdering her husband, however most had deliberately forgotten the girl left behind.

Rosalyn looked up at Elsa. "I haven't been to her grave since they buried her."

Elsa cupped her cheek. "It's okay, Rosie. She understands and so does God. You're doing what you can to survive." She pushed a rag in Rosalyn's hand. "Now clean up that mess and then we can talk."

With a nod, Rosalyn kneeled on the floor and wiped up the milk and glass, emptying it into a bucket Elsa set on the floor. The simple act of cleaning helped Rosalyn focus and get her breath back. She'd had no idea that Elsa had known her mother and the shock had knocked her sideways.

"Now sit down and listen to me." Elsa gave her another glass of milk. "And don't drop this one."

Rosalyn took the glass with shaking hands and drank half of it right away. The sweet liquid tasted wonderful. She glanced up at Elsa who stood with her arms crossed and a frown marring her small face.

"I've been wanting to help you for years but you wouldn't let me. Every time I tried to get close to you, you ran like a rabbit." A ghost of a smile touched her lips. "You look just like Marilyn when she was a young woman."

Rosalyn resisted the urge to feel her face, to find her mother. "Is that good?"

Elsa shrugged. "I think so. You're as beautiful as she was. You also remind the town of what they did, what they shouldn't have done." The frown returned. "I want you to live here and work at the restaurant."

Fear skittered down Rosalyn's back. "I can't stay here. People hate me."

"I don't care. Your mother was my friend and I owe both of you more than the best slops in town." Elsa cleared her throat. "I don't want to force you, Rosie, but I will if I have to."

The determination on the older woman's face told Rosalyn that she meant every word of it. A place to live and this heavenly kitchen were almost appealing. However, her heart ached for another place, another person to call her own.

"Can my cat come live here too?" Rosalyn wouldn't want to leave Whiskers behind.

"I'll feed her, but she'll have to sleep outside. I've got an old crate we can set up for her bed." Elsa frowned. "At least we won't have too many critters nibbling at the food with a cat around."

"Thank you." Rosalyn's mind drifted to the one person she couldn't stop thinking about.

"I know the sheriff is on your mind. I won't come between you, but for now, stay with me. Dickinson is watching him like a hawk, and I've seen Seeger and his thugs hanging around town too much too." Elsa wagged her finger. "It's not safe for you to be alone."

Although it seemed impossible, Rosalyn felt that Elsa truly cared what happened to her. It had been so long, *so long* since anyone had cared she even existed, and now this. Two people had demonstrated that the world wasn't always a dark place. A small spear of light shone on her.

"Can I go visit him whenever I want to?" As she gulped more milk, her entire body shook with the force of impending change.

Elsa really smiled this time. "He comes in here for three meals a day. If you need to see him any more than that, you might as well marry him."

℘

The sun shone brightly on Monday as Noah walked to Elsa's. He hadn't given up on finding Rosalyn, but he had concentrated on being the sheriff. His days had been full of drunks, a few petty thefts and one prank on an outhouse that made him laugh so hard he almost hurt himself. Rosalyn would have laughed even harder.

As he passed the telegram office, he heard a whistle. He poked his head in the door.

"You've got a reply to one of your telegrams, Sheriff." Kenneth Smith held out a piece of yellow paper.

Noah snatched it as nicely as he could and tipped his hat. "Much obliged, Smith."

He dashed out the door and opened the telegram. His worst fears were realized. Seeger had lied about his land boundaries. The five hundred acres he claimed were his actually belonged to Finley. Perhaps Seeger was confused. No, not possible. He had been crystal clear about the acreage, maybe hoping Noah would be as docile as Sheriff Boyton.

Seeger was mistaken. Noah wouldn't let one rancher take advantage of another for any reason. There was too much ugliness in the world to allow it to continue if he could do something to stop it.

A memory of his real mother burst into his head, of her doing what she had to do to survive, on her knees for the man she worked for. Noah closed his eyes and willed away the image.

He should've kept his eyes open. Before he could react, two men yanked him into the alley behind the hotel, and in the shadows, started beating him, using fists, boots and what Noah thought was a club. Pain speared through him as he fought against them. They'd punched him in the eyes first, making it even harder to see.

He reached for his gun, but it wasn't in the holster. Agony exploded when they kicked him in the balls. He couldn't catch his breath, could only will away the black spots dancing behind his eyes.

"Bastard. You think you can come in here and be part of this town? You ain't even lived here a'fore."

He recognized the voice, but couldn't place it. However, the man's sentiment was well known to Noah—he'd heard it many times before. As a hand reached down to cover his mouth, he clamped hold of it and bit as hard as he could while he kicked out. Noah fought like an animal, the fear and fury warring within him. The coppery taste of blood coated his tongue and he knew he'd caused at least a bit of pain to his attacker.

"Fuck! He won't let go of my hand," the first one complained.

The second one kicked him in the kidneys and Noah knew a moment where he thought he was going to pass out from the anguish. Again and again the boot landed on his back. He flipped over and let go of the hand in his mouth, only to feel another crunch his bones with a stone-hard fist.

Amidst the grunts and curses, he heard a howling meow and a hiss, and something that sounded like a screaming banshee. The screech echoed through the alley and Noah thanked God for whatever spirits were watching over him.

"What the hell was that? Sounds like a goddamn ghost."

The smell of tobacco and cheap whiskey floated past Noah's nose. His attacker leaned in closer.

"Do what you're told, boy, or this will seem like a Sunday school kiss."

Noah lurched forward and head-butted the man, earning a hot spray of blood on his face. Boots scraped and curses littered the air. The banshee screeched again and within seconds the men were gone.

Every inch of his body throbbed, some more than others. He spat out a mouthful of the other man's blood and swallowed the bile that rose from the taste. A small coarse tongue started licking his face. Noah focused on a calico cat staring at him with golden eyes.

"My angel?" he said rustily.

"Sheriff Calhoun, looks like you need my help after all. Your deputy is back." Rosalyn's image danced in front of his eyes, then a rush of blackness overwhelmed him.

Chapter Eight

With Elsa's help, and some kindly folks from the restaurant, they carried Noah back to the jail. The town doctor, Eldred Ramsey, arrived and Rosalyn stayed downstairs while he tended to Noah. He'd looked awful, covered in blood with swollen eyes and what she thought was a broken nose. Marina and Elsa paid Doctor Ramsey and he left without even glancing at Rosalyn.

Elsa had been right. The town ignored her intentionally— she was a painful reminder of what a mob could and would do. Whiskers wound her way around Rosalyn's legs, seemingly content to be indoors.

"Will you be all right?" Marina's gaze was filled with concern.

Rosalyn frowned. "I'll be fine."

Elsa moved beside her and clapped Rosalyn on the back so hard she stumbled. "Rosie is a tough girl. She can survive anything."

Marina frowned. "Rosie?"

"Never mind. She'll be staying with me from now on and working in the restaurant." Elsa leveled a hard gaze at Rosalyn. "Isn't that right, missy?"

Regardless if she'd made up her mind or not, Elsa apparently thought it was going to be true. "Yeah, that's right."

Marina took her hands. "You are welcome to stay at the saloon with me too. I know it's not as respectable as Elsa's, but the door is always open."

Rosalyn bit her lip to stop herself from asking why Marina was being so nice to her. Instinct made her distrustful of anyone and anything until she had reason to trust them. So far, a good reason hadn't come along. She stepped away from Marina and stuck her hands behind her back.

"Thanks. I, uh, appreciate it." Rosalyn glanced at Elsa. "I ain't taking charity now. Whatever I eat or sleep in I aim to earn."

Both of the other women nodded. Rosalyn felt like they were funning with her, but didn't want to hurt their feelings if she was wrong.

"I'll bring you both some dinner in a couple hours." Elsa pointed upstairs. "Take care of him today. Tomorrow you can start work."

After Elsa left, Marina approached Rosalyn and sighed. "I know you don't trust me and that's okay. Once upon a time, I was living on the streets of Kansas City. A much bigger, meaner place than here. Someone took a chance on me and gave me the opportunity to go west. I've been you."

A lump formed in Rosalyn's throat at the honesty she saw in Marina's eyes.

"It's okay. You don't have to say anything." With one last squeeze to Rosalyn's shoulder, Marina left her alone.

So many things, changes, challenges, confusion. Rosalyn could hardly take it all in. The quiet in the jail after everyone had gone was comforting. She heard the muffled sounds of the street and closed her eyes, breathing deeply.

If she was going to take what Noah, Elsa and Marina offered, then she needed to do it on her own terms. There was no way she'd survive by someone else's rules. She had to live by her own. Whiskers meowed, her golden eyes wisely confirming Rosalyn's decision.

Although she appreciated Elsa's offer, working in the restaurant didn't appeal to Rosalyn. Except of course for eating in the kitchen. What she really wanted to do was be Noah's deputy. She liked the idea of helping people, but she understood Marina's concern about folks not accepting a woman deputy.

Rosalyn would just have to be a man instead. That was it exactly. She was thin enough, so maybe if she dressed like a man, people would be more apt to accept her as a deputy.

The idea firmly planted in her mind, Rosalyn crept into Noah's room to fetch his extra shirt and britches. She tried not to look at him lying on the bed, but her eyes were drawn to him as if she couldn't control herself. His brown hair was tousled on the pillow, sinfully long eyelashes gracing his bruised cheeks. His swollen lips appeared almost in a pout. Rosalyn was halfway to the bed before she realized what she was doing.

She shook her head at her own stupidity. She'd never been foolish before meeting Noah Calhoun. As quietly as she could, she took the extra clothes hanging on hooks on the wall. Rosalyn had to force herself not to look at him again. He was hurt and needed sleep, not to be peeped at when he was most vulnerable.

After she got back downstairs, she slipped off her brown dress and put Noah's clothes on. The dadgum pants were a foot too wide, so she ended up using a length of rope to hold them up. The cat batted at the swinging ends until Rosalyn shooed her away.

She frowned at her brown shoes held together with spit and string. Even though they weren't feminine looking, they didn't look like a man's boots either, but they'd have to do. She knew Noah's boots would never fit her, and besides, he only had the one pair.

Rosalyn wished she had a mirror to see what she looked like. Something wasn't right but she couldn't put her finger on it.

Her hair! That was the problem. She held her hair up for scrutiny. Even though she'd had a bath a week earlier, her hair already had bits of dirt and leaves in it. It would be better if she didn't have to worry about long hair at all.

Rosalyn went back upstairs to get Noah's knife.

℘

Noah woke suddenly as if someone had pinched him awake. Pain washed through him in a slow agonizing roll. He sucked in a breath then let it out with the least amount of effort. His ribs hurt, but he vaguely remembered the doctor telling him nothing was broken.

That in itself was a miracle. He'd lived through worse, but it had been a hell of a beating. There wasn't much on him that didn't ache or throb. He rubbed his eyes gently to clear away the sleep.

He smelled Rosalyn. Her natural clean scent seemed to be permanently stuck in his nose. The memory of a cat licking his face and Rosalyn standing over him in the alley made him sit upright in the bed. His breath left his body in a whoosh as every piece of him reminded him quite painfully that he couldn't and shouldn't move that fast.

Rosalyn had been there, in the alley. He remembered now. She'd had a calico cat with her that meowed like a little coyote. The rest of it was a bit of a blur, but she had saved him.

By his estimate it must've been the middle of the day, but someone had hung a blanket over the window to block out the sun. Sunlight peeked around the corners, pricking his eyes with its shine.

"Rosalyn?" he called out into the darkened room.

A scrape on the stairs told him someone was walking up. The door opened just a crack.

"Noah?"

Relief washed through him that she was *there*.

"I'm awake."

She entered the room and quickly closed the door behind her. The shadows barely outlined her figure. Something, however, seemed wrong.

She cleared her throat. "How are you feeling?"

"Like I got run over by a horse, but I'm alive. I've got you to thank for that." He touched his nose gingerly. "I'm thankful, Rosalyn."

"It wasn't nothing, really. That's what a deputy does, right?" She stepped closer to the bed.

Noah heard something in her voice that gave him pause. "What's the matter?"

"Um, I have something to show you. Don't get mad."

Noah had no idea what she was talking about, but his gut churned with anxiety. She pulled the blanket back from the window and Noah blinked at the sudden bright light.

"I just wanted to be your deputy."

As she walked toward the bed, Noah felt completely confused. She didn't even look like herself. He closed his eyes then opened them again, sure he'd see something different. Another place, another person rushed through his head. He swallowed back a handful of panic. Rosalyn reminded him so much of himself for a moment, he couldn't get a word past the lump in his throat.

Holy shit.

Rosalyn wasn't Rosalyn anymore. She'd shed the brown dress for his clothes, which hung on her like a child playing dress up, except for her full breasts that seemed out of place. What really made his head pound wasn't the way she was dressed. It was her hair.

Her beautiful black locks had been shorn almost completely off. She'd hacked it up above her ears until it stuck up like a blackbird's tail feathers. Noah was absolutely speechless.

Rosalyn touched her hair. "I know I ain't pretty but leastways folks will think I'm a man now and I can be your deputy."

Noah couldn't stop the tears that pricked his lids. Acceptance had been a hard battle he'd fought all his life. Until the Calhouns found him, he'd never been successful at it. Even after he'd been adopted, the little boy who hid in the shadows of the barn still felt out of place.

He patted the bed next to him and she stepped over hesitantly as if she expected him to hurt her. Noah put his hands on his lap with the fingers twined together and gave her his most innocent expression. She reached the bed then kneeled on the floor beside him.

Slowly he reached out and cupped her cheek. Stiff at first, she finally closed her eyes and leaned into his palm. Noah's heart beat madly with the feelings that whooshed through him. Rosalyn had been a mission for him, something to accomplish, not really a person.

Now she was much more than that. She gave him the most precious gift anyone could give another.

Trust.

"You didn't have to cut your hair," he whispered. "You were already perfect."

Rosalyn opened her violet eyes and searched his gaze. "I'm thinking you need spectacles."

Noah barked out a laugh, trying desperately to control the physical pain and the emotional storm that warred within him.

"Sweet, sweet, Rosalyn." He leaned over and kissed her softly, his ribs protesting every move.

"Does that mean I shouldn't wear your clothes either?" She glanced down at the shirt. "'Cause the britches are mighty big for me."

"No, sweetheart. You probably shouldn't." He pressed his lips to her forehead, inhaling her scent and recognizing that he was falling fast and hard.

Her eyes narrowed. "What did you call me?"

This time the pain be damned, Noah couldn't let the moment pass. He held her face in his hands and looked into her eyes.

"I called you sweetheart. My love, my sweet, my heart." His mouth leaned down towards hers and she met him halfway.

Noah's heart soared as it recognized his true mate, the one he'd been looking for all his life. The other half of his soul.

He'd fallen in love.

"Where in the heck is everybody?" Elsa called from downstairs.

Rosalyn's wary gaze told him that she might trust him, but not enough. Noah wasn't surprised, nor was he expecting more yet. He kissed her quickly.

"Up here, Elsa," he replied.

Elsa clunked up the stairs and came into the bedroom with a frown. "You shouldn't be up here alone, Rosie. Folks are already talking about you and the sheriff."

"I was just talking." Rosalyn rose to her feet.

Elsa whistled when she got close enough to see Rosalyn. "Holy Jesus, girl. What have you done?"

"I asked her to cut her hair," Noah lied. "If she's going to live on the streets, it's better if it's short."

"That's a whopper if I ever heard one." Elsa glared. "She's not living on the streets no more but I guess she didn't tell you that yet, did she? Rosie is going to live and work at the restaurant."

Noah hid his disappointment. Although she wasn't the ideal deputy, Rosalyn had something others didn't. Heart and passion, not to mention determination and the will to survive. She'd make an excellent lawman, or lawwoman, if there was such a thing.

"Get out of his clothes right quick a'fore someone sees you." Elsa shooed Rosalyn out of the room. "I found that blue dress in the desk drawer. Put that on."

If she had wanted to respond, Rosalyn didn't have the chance. Elsa was a force of nature when she wanted to be, even if she didn't stand five feet tall. She turned back to Noah.

"Don't break that girl's heart."

"I wasn't planning on it." Noah fought the urge to slide down onto the bed as exhaustion crept over him.

"Hmph. Well, just so you know she's under my protection now. I've an obligation to that girl I've ignored for ten years." Elsa brought over a basket and the scent of fresh bread tickled his nose. "Here's your dinner. You gonna be able to eat by yourself?"

Noah had a feeling Elsa would offer to feed him and he'd end up with more bruises than he started with. "Yes, ma'am. I believe I can manage it."

"Good, 'cause I'm taking her with me, see if I can fix that hair. Jehoshaphat, that girl is a wild thing. Who put it in her head to cut her hair like that?"

Elsa set the basket down and he spotted some cold chicken, two biscuits and a jar of milk.

Noah's stomach rumbled. "She just wants to fit in, to be accepted."

"That's what I figured." Elsa laid a napkin on top of the food. "Foolish girl. Ain't no one going to accept her if she dresses like a man."

"What she needs to understand is that it doesn't matter what they think." Noah's voice caught. "It's what she thinks that matters." It was a lesson he hadn't learned until he was almost Rosalyn's age.

Elsa looked into his eyes for a long moment before she nodded. "You're a wise man, Noah Calhoun. I expect life hasn't been kind to you either. Just remember that she's like a wounded bird, apt to fly away if you hold her too tightly."

Noah didn't respond. He couldn't. What was he going to say, that he loved her? Elsa probably wouldn't believe it and would try to keep them apart. He'd just be patient and keep his arms open, waiting for his blackbird to fly to him.

&

Over the next two days, Rosalyn snuck in to see him every chance she could. It was as if she couldn't stop herself. After being away from him, instead of the feelings for Noah fading, they'd actually grown stronger. Elsa must've known what was going on, but she didn't say anything.

It was three in the afternoon when Rosalyn made it over to the jail, a basket with peaches and biscuits in her hand. She stepped into the building and leaned against the door, sure she was loco. How else could she explain her constant urge to be with Noah?

Her instincts were telling her to protect herself, but her heart was singing a different song. He needed her and that made Rosalyn feel ten feet tall. It made her spirits soar and put a constant smile on her face. For the first time in her life, someone needed *her*.

As she walked up the stairs, she heard a thump and a crash.

"Dammit!"

Rosalyn dashed up the last steps and ran into the bedroom. Noah lay on the floor like a turtle that had flipped on his back and couldn't get up. He turned his head when he spied her.

"I'm glad you're here, but I'm embarrassed to be caught like this." He gusted out a breath. "Can you help me, sweetheart?"

Rosalyn set down the basket and helped Noah back into the bed. He groaned when he leaned back against the pillows. She cupped his cheek as a surge of tenderness whipped through her.

"Did you think you were ready to run around the building?" she teased as her thumb rasped across his whiskers.

"No, just around the room." He sighed. "I lost my balance when I turned, my head got all dizzy and then the floor decided it needed me."

Rosalyn chuckled. "Did you hurt yourself?"

"Just my pride." Noah turned his head and kissed her palm. "You smell good."

Her heart beat so fast, she was afraid he'd be able to hear it. Confusion and need argued within her. Rosalyn decided the best thing to do was to listen to her instincts and follow her heart.

She leaned forward and kissed him gently. "You don't."

Noah barked a laugh then clutched the side of his head. "Ooh, that hurt. You make me feel better just by being here."

Rosalyn smiled. "I can wash you up if you'd like."

Noah's eyes darkened with need and hunger. "I don't want to make you do anything you don't want to."

"I never let anyone make me do anything."

He licked his lips. "Where's Elsa?"

"With her friends drinking coffee." Rosalyn's body thrummed with excitement. "Should I get the soap and water?"

Noah nodded with a jerk as his gaze slid to her nipples. Rosalyn knew they were hard so she didn't bother to hide them. It was okay if he knew about it. After all, they'd already been with each other before.

This time, it would only be a bath, nothing else. Rosalyn wasn't ready for more. Yet.

№

The moonlight streamed through the window, illuminating the room in silver. Sleep eluded Noah. As hard as he tried, he could not turn off his thoughts. They tumbled around like rocks in a can, banging off each other and his head. As he gazed out the window at the night sky, he wondered if he'd ever find the peace he craved. After Rosalyn washed him that afternoon, he simply could not get her out of his thoughts.

He didn't hear the door open, but her scent washed over him just before her cool hands touched his bare shoulders. Noah closed his eyes as a shiver wormed its way down his skin.

"Rosalyn," he whispered.

"I couldn't sleep." She kissed the center of his back. "I need you."

Noah smiled at his reflection in the glass. "I need you too, sweetheart."

"I want to be with you again." She put her hand on his chest. "I think you do too, but I ain't gonna risk my heart on a man who pushes me away."

He choked a laugh. "I don't think I can push you away, Rosalyn. More than that, I don't want to push you away. You are in my heart."

Noah thought he saw her eyes glisten in the darkness, but she leaned forward and kissed him, her lithe tongue coming out to tease his lips.

"Are you sure? This is the last chance."

"I'm sure. Never been more sure of anything in my life." He put his fingers to her lips. "If you want to be with me, then I am all yours."

Her warm lips trailed along his back from one shoulder to the other, leaving a line of goose bumps in their wake. When she cupped his behind, his cock jumped in the flimsy drawers he wore. Just a mere touch and his body stood at the ready for her. A low throb began in his balls as his pulse thrummed to her tune.

Two days after the beating, he was still sore as hell, but it wasn't about to stop him this time. He needed to feel her, touch her, be with her minus her constant chaperones. Marina and Elsa seemed to feel the need to protect Rosalyn from him so she'd been sneaking in to see him, looking like a thief. He didn't want that for her, for them.

Tonight, she was his. He whirled around and pulled her to him. Chest against chest, muscle against muscle. He'd gotten used to her short hair, and although he missed its silky texture on him, the cut accentuated the beautiful lines of her face.

He lowered his mouth to hers and kissed her slowly, licking and nibbling his way from one end of her lips to the other. She moaned deep in her throat and the sound was like a kick to his gut. The first time they'd made love, he wondered if she did it in gratitude without finding pleasure of her own.

This time, Noah's body took over and he was determined to bring them both to a place where no one and nothing could touch them. He slid his tongue into her mouth, leisurely stroking and teasing her as he pressed his hardness into the welcoming softness of her belly.

When her hand cupped him, he started like a greenhorn in a whorehouse. She slid down his body, and a flash of panic lanced through him. Noah pulled her back up until they were chest to chest again, forcing away the bad thoughts that tried to intrude. She seemed to understand what he couldn't or wouldn't do.

"Touch me." Rosalyn put his hand on her breast.

Noah wasn't about to say no. He palmed the perfect orb, feeling its weight, its texture beneath the cotton chemise she wore. He reached down and pulled the hem up over her head, then she was deliciously nude. The heat of her skin almost singed his palm when he found her distended nipple. He pinched and teased the peak, feeling the answering shudders racing through her.

"Now touch me here." She led his hand down to her pussy, and the soft wiry hair tickled his palm.

Wetness coated his fingers as he slid against her. She grunted when he put two fingers inside her, gliding in even as his palm continued to tease her clit. If he wasn't careful, he'd make himself come simply by touching her.

Her small hands closed around him beneath his drawers. She seemed to have the knack for his pleasure spots because at once, she gripped the base and squeezed the tip—a double round of heaven that distracted him from pleasuring her.

Noah leaned down and captured one breast in his mouth. Sucking and licking, he timed his tongue's laps with his fingers' movement. She started moving with him, pushing against his hand and his mouth. He'd definitely distracted her because her hands on his cock loosened. It was enough for him to breathe and focus on her.

"Come on, sweetheart, come." He nibbled at her nipple then with one last lick, switched sides.

When his lips closed around the second nipple, she trembled and Noah knew she was close. He put a third finger inside her and bit her, fucking her with his hand until she exploded against him.

Rosalyn cried out, a primitive female sound that echoed through his bones. After the tremors ceased, he scooped her up and nearly ran to the bed. He set her down with a fierce kiss, then pulled off his drawers so hard, he heard a seam pop.

She opened her arms and welcomed him to her body. A sigh escaped as they touched from top to bottom. She was so soft, like an angel beneath him. His heart couldn't take much more waiting, not to mention the rest of him begging for release.

"Rosalyn, I—"

"Shhhh." She pressed her fingers to his lips. "Love me."

He pushed into her just an inch, then withdrew, his body screaming in protest. It had been so messy and so fast before, he wanted to savor every second with her. Another inch and she moaned against his ear.

Torturing himself with turtle-slow speed, he finally sank to the hilt into her body. The hot clench of her muscles around him stole his breath. He sucked on her neck, trying to grasp the edges of his self-control.

"You feel so good," she whispered.

It was as if Noah's tongue forgot how to form words. So he did the only thing he could do, he made love to her with his heart. His thrusts were meant to heighten their pleasure, long, then short, long, then short. He never forgot her breasts, her neck, her ears, her lips. She writhed beneath him, pushing up against him even as he kept his agonizing pace.

"Faster. *Now.*"

Rosalyn's order and a pinch on his ass destroyed the wall of self-control he'd been hiding behind. His body took over and he slammed into her with as much feeling as he had in his heart. Over and over, she cried his name, meeting his fierceness with her own.

"Oh God, oh God." She clawed at his back. "I'm almost there."

So was he. So close he could taste the force of the orgasm about to hit him. He latched onto her lips as it struck. He breathed in her essence as her body accepted his. Stars danced behind his lids and he couldn't imagine a more perfect moment. She groaned low and long in his ear as his heart beat a steady rhythm against hers.

"Noah." A small whisper, full of awe and love.

Noah held her close as tremors wracked his body and tears threatened. It had been much more than making love. It had been the moment his life changed.

℘

Dawn washed the room in its pink light, covering the two of them in its sweet kiss. Rosalyn lay awake, staring at Noah, wondering how she'd gotten to the point where a man was important to her.

More than important, almost required to live. The last three weeks had brought so many changes she could barely keep up with them. The only steady thing had been the man who lay beside her. She wasn't certain what love was, but she had a feeling this was it.

Rosalyn thought about him all the time. Even when she was washing dishes or sweeping the kitchen. She even dreamt of him each night, until she couldn't stand being away from him any longer. Elsa probably knew that Rosalyn had snuck out, but she didn't care.

It had been worth it. Noah had brought her the moon and the stars and everything in between. He'd pleasured her, showed her what a beautiful thing two people could make together. If it wasn't love, then it was definitely like.

She thought about waking him up to do it again, but knew that Elsa would already be cursing and looking for her. They started serving breakfast just after the sun rose, which meant she had about two minutes to get back to the restaurant.

Rosalyn rose quietly and slipped on her dress. She leaned over and kissed him on the lips as softly as a butterfly wing.

"I love you, Noah Calhoun."

Chapter Nine

Decoration Day arrived with a lot of pomp and circumstance. Folks decorated the town in red, white and blue and built a stage for a celebration and dance. The Civil War had seemed far away to people in Wyoming, but the urge to celebrate those who had died ran strong. Many had settled there after the war, bringing with them the tales of the bloodiest times in American history.

Five years earlier, the mayor, Bertie Albertson, declared that Decoration Day would always have a celebration and dance. It was Mayor Dickinson's first Decoration Day but he kept with the tradition and the celebration was planned.

Noah observed it all, waiting for the opportunity to connect Dickinson with Seeger and his dirty dealings. He knew he was being watched and because he was still recovering from his wounds, he dared not confront the cattle rancher yet.

Each night Rosalyn came to him and they made sweet love. Each morning she left before the sun rose. This morning had been different though. He'd been awake, already hard with need for her, but she'd scrambled out of bed before he could move. Working for Elsa gave her pride and he understood that all too well. Noah played possum and let her leave.

But not before she'd kissed his forehead and whispered that she loved him. Noah felt frozen, unable to utter a sound as she walked out of the bedroom.

She loved him?

When did that happen? She didn't even know him, not the real him. Noah knew he needed to be completely honest with her, brutally honest, before Rosalyn stepped from the shadows of her own world into the burning darkness of his.

He trembled with the urge to go find her at Elsa's. Instead, he helped with the preparations for the picnic and dance. His ribs still hurt, but he could carry cake and cookies to the dessert table and shoo away boys who hovered nearby hoping for a sweet treat.

Chancetown seemed normal for once. No anxiety or rancor peppered the air. Decoration Day brought people together like nothing else did. He knew it was an illusion, that beneath the surface the underbelly of avarice lurked.

Dinnertime brought everyone to socialize, eat and gossip. Noah walked amongst them greeting people, meeting those he hadn't met before and keeping an eye on the happenings.

"Sheriff Calhoun, fancy meeting you here," Mrs. Knudsen's singsong rang out.

Noah cursed silently. He'd completely forgotten about Mrs. Knudsen's matchmaking schemes. Pity on him for not being more alert. He turned to find her and her daughter wearing identical red, white and blue dresses with matching bonnets. All that was missing was the flag poles on their backs.

"Mrs. Knudsen, Josephine." He tipped his hat. "You both look festive."

"Well, we want to celebrate our soldiers just like everyone else." Mrs. Knudsen tittered. "I had a feeling we'd run into you at the dance. You will save one for Josephine, right?"

How to say no without offending them? It wasn't their fault Noah was obsessed with Rosalyn, that he couldn't go five minutes without wondering where she was and what she was doing. It wasn't fair to them to allow Mrs. Knudsen to think Noah was even remotely interested in her daughter.

He opened his mouth to tell her, but instead he said, "I'm working tonight, ma'am. As I told you, it's my job to make sure things are orderly."

Noah murmured a polite goodbye and disappeared into the crowd. He felt their eyes on his back and cursed himself for not being honest with them. His gaze continued to search the crowd for one dark-haired woman.

"She's not here yet." Marina spoke from beside him.

Noah glanced down at his friend. "Who?"

She snorted. "I'm not stupid, you know. I see the way you look at Rosalyn and I've also seen the way she looks at you. Be careful."

Unbelievably, he felt hurt by Marina's warning. "I won't hurt her. More than likely she'll hurt me. She's run away from me before, you know." Realizing he sounded petulant, Noah shut his mouth before he sounded even more like an idiot.

Marina raised one dark brow. "So that's the way of it, hmm? You'll be good for each other." She hooked her arm through his. "Escort me over to the table so I can get some cake and lemonade without any dirty looks."

Noah chuckled. "Lady in distress?"

"Something like that." A shadow passed over her face, but it was gone in a second.

"Your wish is my command." He grinned, and for a short time was content to be with his friend and eat a sweet treat.

The sun set before he saw Rosalyn. Dressed in her blue dress with a matching blossom tucked into her black locks, she was the stuff of dreams. Noah watched with hungry eyes, as did many other men around him. He'd known that bringing her from the streets would put her in danger from unscrupulous men. The lust clearly written on their faces confirmed that fear.

Rosalyn needed him.

He nodded politely to the men he'd been speaking to and sauntered over to Rosalyn just as four young bucks surrounded her.

"Why hello there, miss. I don't believe we've met. I'm Wentworth Jones," a blond one said, hat crushed to his chest.

Another one, this one with red hair, pushed his friend aside. "Why don't be taken in by that fool, miss. I'm Elmer Boudreau. Pleased to meet you."

"Boys!" Noah barked, startling the lot of them. "Miss Benedict is under my protection. Y'all need to be on your way."

All four glanced back and forth between Noah's scowl and Rosalyn's beauty. At least two of them probably considered telling him to go to hell, but in the end, they slunk away with promises of buggy rides and Sunday afternoon dinners.

Rosalyn's expression never changed. The hunted animal never lost its instincts and she understood the young men were scenting her for a mate. However, more than likely once they found out who she really was, all they'd want from her was an easy fuck. The very thought of anyone using her like that made Noah want to beat his chest and howl at the moon. He wanted to keep her safe, make her happy, make her realize what an amazing person she was.

Noah whipped off his hat and sketched a short bow. "Miss Rosalyn, you look...stunning."

Her eyes were the same color as her dress and he felt himself falling into them. The sound of fiddles warming up and a drumbeat echoed behind them. He held out his hand, the palm wet with leftover anger for the men who would use her. Noah tried his damnedest to shake it off and focus on Rosalyn instead of himself.

She never broke his gaze. "Does that mean you think I look pretty?"

"Oh God, Rosalyn, you passed pretty about ten miles back. You're the most beautiful woman here." He breathed out a sigh of relief when she put her gloved hand in his.

"You don't need to butter me up, Noah. I'll still come to your bed."

He smothered a shocked chuckle. "Jesus please us, Rosalyn, you can't say things like that in public. Folks don't look kindly on women who spend their time in bed with a man they're not married to."

She shrugged. "Why do I care what they think?"

Noah struggled to make her understand. "If you want to live here and be part of this town, then you have to follow the rules."

"But we ain't following them." Rosalyn frowned and tugged at his hand. "You're ashamed of me."

Noah realized what he'd been saying to her and could have cut out his own tongue. She was right. They weren't following anybody's rules but their own and it didn't matter one lick what the town thought. If he lost his job, then he'd just find one elsewhere, even if it meant leaving Chancetown. If he was lucky, he would leave with Rosalyn on his arm.

"No, I'm not. I'm ashamed of me." With that, Noah lowered his head and kissed her hard in front of all and sundry.

A few whistles met their ears, but he ignored them. When he lifted his head, her lips glistened with the remnants of their kiss. She smiled and he knew everything was all right.

They stepped onto the dance floor and she glanced around at the other dancers. They were doing a simple square dance, but Rosalyn looked as if she'd never seen such a thing. Noah took hold of her and guided her around the wooden floor. She fit perfectly in his arms and under his chin. Her violet eyes sparkled with joy as they moved in unison to the music.

"Slut!" The ugly word rang like a broken bell.

The music stopped and several couples bumped into each other. Shep Seeger strode out onto the dance floor, his spurs jingling and malice in his eyes. His two thugs stood behind him, wearing smirks on their faces and pistols on their hips. One of them wore a bandage on his hand—no doubt one of the bastards who had jumped him.

"That girl doesn't belong in polite company." He pointed at Rosalyn. "She's as much of a slut as her mother was."

Rosalyn lurched toward the rancher and Noah held her back.

"Don't you talk about my mama." Her teeth bared like a she-wolf protecting her cub.

"Ha! I can talk about her all day." Seeger circled around her. "She was a slut and a murderer. An embarrassment to this town."

A murderer? Rosalyn's mother was a *murderer?* What the hell?

Rosalyn launched herself at Seeger with fists flying. She even got a punch in before Noah grabbed hold of her. Seeger's hand rose but Noah stopped his arm in mid-motion.

"Don't even think about hitting her." Noah's voice shook with fury. "You will never hit a woman while I'm sheriff in this town. No one will."

Seeger's eyes flashed with repressed rage. "You're only the sheriff as long as we let you keep the job."

"Be careful who you threaten, Seeger." Noah felt the weight of everyone's stares as the two of them squared off. He couldn't, wouldn't back down. It wasn't just for Rosalyn, but for himself. Noah had spent too much time cowering from bullies like Seeger. He wasn't ever going to do it again.

Seeger must've seen something in Noah's eyes because he stepped away. "Don't forget what I said, Calhoun." He gestured at Rosalyn. "And get that little bitch off this dance floor." He touched the spot on his cheek where she'd hit him before turning away.

"I believe Mr. Seeger is right. This ah, person doesn't belong at this celebration," Dickinson's nasally voice added from behind them.

Noah spun around, making the mayor step back a pace. The natty man was dressed in his best bowler hat and another brand-new suit.

"Why doesn't she belong here? Is she not American? Does she not deserve to celebrate all those who died during the Civil War?" Noah's words grew louder as he spoke. "It doesn't matter where you came from or what your parents did. Every person should be accepted for who they are and not be judged."

"It's our right to limit the riffraff that comes into this town. We've got good folks here, and we don't need the daughter of a murderer among us." He pointed a pudgy finger at Rosalyn. "She needs to leave."

Noah's heart hammered against his ribs as the blood raced crazily around his body. This was his decision time, when he needed to choose between Rosalyn and his job. He hadn't expected it to happen so soon, but he'd already made up his mind what he was going to say. There wasn't really a choice. A job didn't even begin to compare to a woman like Rosalyn.

As he opened his mouth, Elsa stepped in front of him.

"This is an American celebration and not one person should be excluded." She made sure her icy gaze touched every onlooker. "This girl works for me and she's good people. I wouldn't have hired her if I didn't believe that. You should be ashamed of yourselves, the lot of you. Treating this poor girl like the shit on your shoes." She glanced at Noah. "The sheriff saw the diamond in the rough and gave me a kick in my fanny that I needed. Rosalyn Benedict is as much a citizen of this town as the rest of you. She deserves to be a part of this here party. Anyone who wants to disagree with me can tell me now."

The only sound to be heard was the crickets singing their lullaby in the night air. Rosalyn's breath jumped in and out, her hand trembling in his. Noah squeezed it and finally dared meet her gaze. Hurt, distrust and fury swirled in their violet depths.

"I'm sorry, sweetheart." He meant it from the depths of his soul. People were cruel creatures who fed off others' pain.

She shook her head and started to walk away. Noah wouldn't let go of her hand.

"You're not going anywhere. Elsa's right. You belong here." He took her in his arms again. "Right here."

"What are y'all waiting for? Get to the fiddlin' again. We've got a party to finish." Elsa gestured to the musicians, who one by one picked up their instruments and the music began anew.

Seeger stood in a huddle with his men and Dickinson. That could only mean trouble for Noah and Rosalyn. He had to find a way to determine exactly what was going on in Chancetown and put a stop to it.

Noah saw Mrs. Knudsen and Josephine standing at the edge of the crowd, disappointment on their faces. The young woman looked at Rosalyn almost wistfully before her mother pulled her away. At least he wouldn't have to continue the façade of running from them—the Knudsens already knew his choice had been made. He hated the fact he hadn't been honest with them from the start and would make it a point to apologize to them.

The magic of the night had been broken, yet Rosalyn was still in his arms, albeit a bit reluctantly. Seeger and Dickinson had gone too far and Noah intended that it wouldn't happen again. Protectiveness surged within him for Rosalyn. He meant what he said. It didn't matter who her mother was or what she did, Rosalyn was her own person and deserved the opportunities everyone else got.

It felt like he was holding a board in his arms instead of a woman. She kept her eyes down and her body stiff. When the dance was over, she mumbled a thank you and disappeared into the darkness that had fallen around them.

Marina stepped up beside him. "I'm sorry that happened. I know you were looking forward to being with her tonight."

"I'd like to wring Seeger's neck. Arrogant ass." Just the thought of what the rancher had said made his pulse jump. He'd do his best to track down the man with the bandaged hand too.

"Be careful who you threaten because you never know who's listening." Marina squeezed his arm and walked away, leaving Noah with his thoughts whirling like a dervish.

Tomorrow he'd find out from Elsa exactly who Rosalyn was and what her mother had done. Then he'd be prepared to defend her and keep her by his side. A cool breeze blew and Noah shivered in the springtime night air. He had a feeling this confrontation was only the beginning. There was a lot left to uncover.

ℰℭ

That night Rosalyn didn't come to see him. He spent a lonely night staring at the stars and wondering why he was seeing her face in the twinkling blackness. When the sun rose, he gave up the battle for sleep and got out of bed, ready for an early morning walk.

Downstairs he found a note on the desk from Marina asking him to stop by the saloon to talk. She had information he needed to know. Intrigued, Noah strapped on his gun belt and realized he'd have to wait a few hours to see her. There was no way she was up at the crack of dawn.

Instead, he headed to the restaurant to get information from Elsa. Too many ghosts stood between him and Rosalyn. He aimed to shoo them all away to get to her.

Although it was still mighty early, there were plenty of folks out on the street. By the time he got to the restaurant, he'd been stopped twice and must've said hello at least ten times in the short walk down the street. When he walked inside, others waved and greeted him. He'd no idea who most of them were, but obviously the Decoration Day picnic had made them sit up and take notice of the sheriff.

He was fairly certain it was a good thing, but at the moment he felt a bit uncomfortable with all the attention. After escaping from the townspeople, he went into the kitchen and found Elsa. Lucky for him, Rosalyn was not there.

Elsa was grinding coffee beans when Noah walked in. "I figured I'd see you this morning."

"You figured right." He sat on the stool next to the stove. "Elsa, you need to tell me what you know about Rosalyn. I'm thinking I have a future with that girl but I'll be damned if I can figure her out."

With a deep frown, Elsa studied the coffee grounds in the grinder. "I knew Rosalyn as a child. She had a hard eight years with her family. Maybe if you know more about who she was, you can better understand who she is now. Her daddy, Shug Benedict, was a bully, a man who beat his wife if she even looked at him crosswise. Rosalyn was spared his fists because of her mother. She loved that little girl more than life itself." Elsa met Noah's gaze. "Shug got it in his mind that his daughter was more of a nuisance than anything. He tried to strangle her."

Noah was mesmerized by Elsa's words.

"Marilyn picked up a shotgun and killed her husband that night. By sunrise, the townsfolk had hung her from that cottonwood at the end of the main street. Rosalyn had to watch it all." Elsa shook her head. "People treat Rosalyn as if she doesn't exist or maybe guilt kept them from acknowledging they'd hung a woman whose husband had beaten her daily for ten years. They'd orphaned her, just as surely as if they'd helped Shug Benedict make a fist. After Marilyn died, Sheriff Boyton had her buried in a small grave in the cemetery. He'd always been nice to Rosalyn and her mother, and in death, respected her memory."

Noah swallowed hard against the lump that had grown in his throat. He'd known Rosalyn had endured much by the way she approached life. What he hadn't known was just how bad it had been. His heart bled for her and for her mother.

"Marilyn Benedict was my friend and I did nothing to help her or Rosalyn. I aim to change that and I started by giving her a job. It ain't enough though." Elsa slammed the coffeepot down so hard the grinder fell over. "Well, shit."

"What do you mean it isn't enough?" Noah wanted to help Rosalyn too, and not just for his own purposes. The Calhouns and Malloys had given him a new start on life, which didn't erase the past that still haunted him, but they gave him a future. With Elsa's help, he could do that for Rosalyn too.

Elsa used her hand to brush the grinds into the coffeepot. "The town still ain't accepting her." She glanced up at Noah. "If'n she married the sheriff, they would."

The words rang through Noah's ears. Marry Rosalyn? Hadn't the very thought been lurking in the back of his heart?

"Boy, don't you faint on me." Elsa waved her fingers in front of Noah's face.

He captured her wrist and kissed the back of her hand. "You are a queen among women, Elsa."

Noah never thought he could knock the older woman speechless, but he had. Her cheeks blushed a becoming shade of pink.

"Oh, go on." She pulled her hand back. "I'm too old for you."

He waggled his eyebrows. "So says you."

Elsa cackled. "Get on with you then. You gonna do right by that girl?"

Noah searched inside him for the answer. Truth was he wanted Rosalyn to be his wife, but there were a lot of things they had to clear up before he could marry her. Instinct told him he'd never find another woman who would be a perfect match like she was. He knew it the first time they made love.

"I plan on it. Not today though so don't go gossiping, okay?"

"I'll give you a week, then all bets are off, cowboy." Elsa patted his shoulder. "Now get out there and do your job. This town needs a good cleaning."

&

The saloon was empty of everyone save Marina, Bitsy and Cherry. The girls were sweeping the floor while Marina tallied receipts at the bar, her usual flouncy dress exchanged for a plain dark blue cotton one. She smiled and waved him in.

Bitsy and Cherry were in robes and their faces were bare of makeup. Both of them squealed, dropped their brooms and ran upstairs. Noah shook his head and Marina smiled.

"With the Decoration Day picnic, I closed the saloon last night. First time in a year that I went to sleep before the sun. They don't know what to do with themselves so early in the day." She chuckled and patted the stool next to him. "Have a seat and I'll get you some coffee."

His gritty eyes reminded him that coffee would be an excellent choice. Elsa hadn't offered him any and he'd plumb forgotten about it during their talk. He gratefully accepted a steaming cup from Marina and took a noisy slurp. The hot thick liquid tasted like ambrosia.

"Delicious."

"It's like tar, but I appreciate the compliment." She sat back down next to him. "There's something I wanted to tell you but a promise to a friend stopped me from doing it before now."

She fiddled with the papers on the bar. "Johnny Boyton is a good man, but not perfect. He made some mistakes as sheriff, just like anybody would. I thought you should know that he moved out to a small ranch just outside town the day after you

135

took over as sheriff. I think he was tired of facing what Chancetown had become." She swallowed a gulp of coffee. "Johnny's pretty shrewd and kept information on certain men in this town that allowed him to keep working even long after he should've been sitting on his front porch whittling all day. You finally gave him the option to leave."

Noah sipped at the hot brew, anxious to hear exactly what Johnny had done that guaranteed his job.

Her dark gaze met Noah's. "I promised him I wouldn't tell a soul, but I think the situation has gotten beyond what he expected. I don't think anyone thought Rosalyn and you would... Well, anyway, Johnny made a deal with Dickinson and the town."

"What kind of deal?" Noah would hate to think Johnny had some shady dealings, but human nature being what it was, it wouldn't surprise him.

"Johnny had information about Dickinson and Seeger. Those two apparently did anything and everything they wanted to make money, and Johnny caught them with their hands dirty." Marina shrugged. "He wasn't ready to quit working yet so he told them he would keep it to himself if they let him run the sheriff's office as he wanted to."

"Not for money?" That would surprise Noah. Not many folks blackmailed others without there being money involved.

"No, not for money. He was happiest being a lawman and he passed sixty more than five years ago. Johnny Boyton wanted to feel useful. He also made a deal with them that whoever he hired would keep the job for one year, unless he was killed." Marina tapped Noah's hand with her fingernail. "Did you hear me?"

Noah shook away the cobwebs in his head. "Are you saying that I can't be fired for a year?"

Marina smiled, the crinkles in the corner of her eyes standing out. Noah realized she wasn't wearing any makeup and she was even lovelier without it. "Yep, that's right. I didn't want you to go on thinking you had to choose between Rosalyn and your job. They can't take it away from you. It's in a legal document stored in the county seat. I told you Johnny was smart."

It was as if a great weight had lifted off his shoulders. There was nothing to keep them from being together except Rosalyn's stubbornness. He kissed Marina on the cheek and let out a whoop. Marina shook her head at his antics.

"Just be careful, Noah. Threatened men are like dogs backed into a corner. They'll bite you, even kill you, to get free. Remember, I said you'd keep the job unless you were killed."

Her sobering warning took some of the air out of Noah's sails. He wouldn't put it past Seeger to try and kill the sheriff. Whatever the rancher's reasons were for killing lambs and driving Finley off had yet to be discovered. Marina was right—a desperate man would turn into an animal.

"Thank you, Marina." He kissed her cheek, inhaling the clean scent of woman.

Marina leaned into him and Noah stumbled backwards. The embarrassment on her face told him he hadn't been mistaken.

"I'm sorry. I didn't mean to—"

"Noah, you didn't do anything wrong. You're a handsome man and so full of life." She shrugged, a sad smile on her face. "I just wanted a brief taste of it."

Marina stuck her cup in front of her face and looked into the black depths of the coffee. Noah took it from her and set it down before cupping her face with both hands.

"You're a beautiful, smart woman who any man would be lucky to call his own." He kissed her quickly on the lips. "My heart belongs to someone else or I'd be after you in two shakes of a lamb's tail."

Marina shook her head. "You're a charmer, you know that?"

He stepped back with his thumbs hooked into the top of his britches. "I don't believe I am. I speak only the truth. That's what lawmen are supposed to do." He squeezed her shoulder. "Thank you for telling me all of this. I know you didn't have to."

"Yes I did." This time Marina smiled.

Noah swallowed the last of the coffee and said goodbye to his friend. He had to find out what Johnny Boyton knew.

Chapter Ten

Rosalyn had trouble waking up on Tuesday. The incident at the Decoration Day party had stolen her sleep. She'd only drifted off sometime near dawn, and then slept like the dead for hours. By the look of the sun, it was almost noon. She'd completely missed working breakfast and might have missed most of the dinner crowd.

She splashed tepid water on her face and tried to clear the sleep from her eyes. Her dreams had been frightening and odd, as if she could see her parents alive again, only this time Rosalyn had been the one hanging from the tree. A shiver wormed its way up her body and she dressed hurriedly in her blue dress.

As she stepped from the small room at the top of the stairs, she heard the clink of glasses and plates from below. She tied on the apron Elsa had given her and ran downstairs. The older woman was in the kitchen, serving up beef stew and biscuits.

"I thought maybe I'd have to send the cavalry for you." Elsa picked up the dishes and thrust them at Rosalyn. "I fed your cat already. She was meowing to wake the dead. Go give these to Martha and Reginald Stevens—they're at the table by the door."

Rosalyn stared in horror at the steaming food. She hadn't yet had to serve any food, had only been working in the kitchen cleaning up and helping.

"No one is going to hurt you, child. Now move it." Elsa frowned and waved her hand. "Earn your keep."

With more than a little fear, Rosalyn stepped into the dining area. The plates trembled in her hands and she prayed to God she wouldn't drop them. She spotted the couple, a young man and his wife, at the same time they spotted her. Rosalyn didn't know them although she had a feeling they knew who she was.

It didn't matter if they did. Rosalyn knew there was nothing to be frightened of. She'd lived so long hiding from people she imagined things that weren't there. Thrusting her shoulders back and clenching her stomach against the fear, Rosalyn walked toward the couple. She even put a small smile on her face.

"Good afternoon, folks." She set the plates down without spilling any. "Enjoy."

The woman murmured a thank you and the man nodded, then they turned their attention toward their food. Rosalyn returned to the kitchen with a huge grin and a spring in her step. Elsa thrust two more plates at her.

"Here. Bring those to the sisters Beddington. They're the two old ladies in the corner."

Rosalyn wasn't completely unafraid of the two biggest gossips in town, but she had confidence she'd survive. She could make it through anything.

∞

Noah rode out to Johnny's small farm at a slow pace using Marina's directions. He thought long and hard about how to talk to the older man, to get the most information without sounding like Noah was interrogating him. Tyler Calhoun had taught him well and Noah aimed to use those skills for the first time.

The sheriff had retired to ten acres a few miles outside town. It was a beautiful place with a lot of trees and a few chickens pecking outside. He heard the low of a cow and the shuffling of a horse or two. Bees buzzed on the wildflowers blooming in the field next to the yard.

As he approached the ranch, Johnny came out of the house wearing a faded pair of overalls and a brown shirt. His straw hat had a cockeyed brim and a few stains.

"I figured I'd see you sooner or later." He frowned. "You'd best come on in then and do your speaking."

Perhaps Johnny assumed Marina would tell Noah about his deal with the town, or maybe the old sheriff had confidence that Noah would figure out something was wrong in town. Either way, at least Noah wouldn't have to start from scratch with his questions. Johnny might even be willing to talk.

Noah tied up his horse outside and followed the older man into the house—a tidy little place with a rag rug, two chairs and a table. The fireplace was surrounded by a bed and a rocking chair. It wasn't much, but at one point in his life, would have been a palace for Noah.

"Coffee?" Johnny held up a battered coffeepot.

"No thanks. I've had enough today." Noah pulled out a chair and sat down, folding his hands on his belly.

Johnny made a big deal of pouring himself a cup, then getting the sugar tin down and spooning some of the sweetness into the coffee. By the time he sat down, Noah had already figured that Johnny was using his own techniques to throw the conversation off before it got started.

Wily old man.

"What can I do for you, Calhoun?"

Noah chose his words carefully. "I've found out some things the past two weeks that have me puzzled. I was hoping you'd be able to help me figure them out."

Johnny's eyebrows rose. "I'd be happy to."

"Someone has been killing Finley's lambs and leaving the bodies for him to find. I expect it's Shep Seeger, but I can't prove it yet. Did you see anything like that when you were the sheriff?" Noah had a feeling Johnny wouldn't admit to it even if he had. Perhaps Seeger had added to the sheriff's coffers on a regular basis.

"Now I can't rightly say I saw any dead lambs." Johnny studied his coffee. "Finley did come to see me a couple of times about some missing sheep. You know those wooly creatures, dumb as stumps. Probably wander off all the time."

"Did you investigate Finley's claims?"

"Nah, didn't have to. He was new in town, didn't know the terrain. Probably lost them himself." Johnny took a long gulp of his coffee.

It was what Johnny didn't say that Noah heard. The former sheriff had known someone was making off with Finley's herd one sheep at a time, but didn't do anything about it. Noah had to tread very lightly.

"He seems like he is very precise and exacting to me. He knew exactly how many sheep he had, how much each one is worth and even knew the boundaries of his land." Noah traced a knot on the table with his finger.

"And you believed him?"

"I believe the land office at the county seat." Noah met Johnny's gaze. "They confirmed what Finley told me."

Noah let Johnny digest that information before continuing. "I think Seeger is playing a very dangerous game and he needs to be stopped. Are you willing to help me, Boyton? Or are you going to hide out here on this farm?"

Johnny's face paled a bit. "There's proof about the land boundaries?"

"Of course there is. Everything can be found if you know where to look." Noah gazed at the older man, willing him to meet his gaze. He was hoping Johnny would be the good man Noah thought he was and own up to his own failings as sheriff.

"I never thought to check with the county." Johnny stood abruptly. "I need more coffee."

Noah knew he hadn't even drunk half the cup, so he was fairly certain the information had rattled Johnny a lot. This was a good thing. A rattled man was more easily swayed.

"Johnny, I know you think you're good and truly stuck here, but that's not true. If we work together we can stop whatever Seeger's doing and make things right." Noah hoped like hell Marina was right about her friend.

Johnny stood with his back to Noah and blew out a breath. "I don't know if I can help you."

Noah rose. "Yes, you can. Marina told me about your deal with Dickinson. Tell me everything you know and maybe between the two of us, we can figure out what to do."

It was a topsy-turvy feeling to be the one planning and pushing for change. He'd always shied away from being up front and in the spotlight. Yet here he was, fighting for his new town.

Johnny's gaze finally met Noah's. "I guess if'n I go to jail, I'll probably die quick." He shrugged. "Maybe I can make some amends for what I done before I meet St. Peter."

Noah held out his hand. "Thank you."

"Don't thank me yet, boy, it's a hard row we're going to have to hoe. You sure you're ready?" Boyton's watery eyes reflected fear and resignation as he shook Noah's hand.

"I'm ready. Just tell me the truth." Noah sat back down.

Johnny landed in the chair with a thump. "It started about ten years back when the first sheep rancher came into Chancetown. Fella by the name of Spiegel. He brung in about a thousand of those wooly creatures, stunk something awful. Spiegel didn't keep 'em on his land either. They ended up eating half the pastureland around Shep's ranch and his cattle were skinny that fall. He only fetched half the price for them and was mighty angry about it."

"I can understand being angry. What happened to Spiegel?" Noah had a feeling he already knew the answer.

"Spiegel liked to drink. One night he drank too much down at the saloon and broke his neck falling off his horse on the way home. Seeger slaughtered the sheep and sold the wool and meat. He kept the profit and made sure Spiegel's widow left." Johnny looked at his trembling hands. "It was another three years before another sheepman came in. Marsters was different than Spiegel, but kept to himself. When something happened to his herd, nobody listened to him or believed him because no one even knew who he was. I did, but I pretended like I didn't. You see, by then Seeger knew he needed me, so he gave me part of the profits from the sheep."

Shame crept into the old sheriff's voice. Noah had no patience for what greed did to men or what they justified in the name of money. Marina obviously didn't have the entire story of what Johnny had done.

"Two more sheepmen came through over the next seven years. They only lasted a few months before Seeger drove them out. I think that bastard Spiegel turned Seeger so badly against them sheep that nothing was gonna change his mind. Then after Finley settled in, Seeger started right in on him." Johnny wiped his eyes on his sleeve. "Finley was different though—he hung on for over a year. I knew it was going to end in blood and didn't want to be a part of it anymore."

"So you plucked me from the saloon and threw the problem in my lap without any warning." Noah's slumbering anger at the old sheriff surged anew. "How does Dickinson fit into Seeger's hatred for sheep ranchers?"

Johnny looked like he might burst into tears. "Dickinson bullied himself into being mayor. He's Seeger's cousin. I think Seeger figured that with someone over the town who he could manipulate, he could prevent sheep ranchers from even buying property. No matter what they did, Finley wouldn't budge." His gaze pleaded with Noah for understanding. "I didn't know what to do and I can't fight those two. They're young bucks and I'm an old fool. When I heard you was a Calhoun... Well, I had a feeling you could do something."

Noah shook his head. "What about your deal with Dickinson and Seeger?"

"Oh that. Yeah, I made that deal before I told them I'd hired you. They thought I was just gonna go look for a new sheriff. Seeger was mighty angry when he found out about you." Johnny ran a hand down his face.

"First of all, there's no guarantee they won't fire me. Second, they could just as easily kill me and put some fool in the sheriff's job who can't find his ass with both hands." Noah's voice rose as his frustration let loose. "You set me up to die, Johnny. I was hoping to really make a difference in this town and meanwhile you were hiding behind dirty dealings and throwing me to the wolves." Noah stood, knocking his chair over. "I'm sorry I came out here. But at least now I know who to tell my parents to hunt after I'm killed."

Panic colored Johnny's face. "No, that's not true. Don't tell your pa to come after me. I didn't do anything."

"Liar." Noah leaned in so close he could see the flecks of fear in Johnny's eyes. "I'm going to do my damnedest to fix this mess you made. If I can arrest Seeger and Dickinson you had better be there to testify against them or I swear to God I'll kill you myself."

Noah left the small cabin and sucked in a deep breath of fresh air. The atmosphere inside had been stifling to the point of making his stomach hurt. He'd known something was wrong, but he hadn't known how deeply the law had been involved with the dirty dealings.

Johnny had been right about one thing. It was going to be a tough row to hoe. Noah mounted his horse and headed back to town, back to think and plan, back to the one person who kept him focused.

એ

Rosalyn finished the dinner dishes by three o'clock. She hadn't slept well the night before, with missing Noah like she did. It had been painful to have folks staring at her while that stupid man called her names. She'd wanted to hurt him as much as he hurt her. Noah had stopped her and for that, Rosalyn was angry with him.

Truth be told, she had almost gone to him for their nightly lovemaking. Elsa had seen her leaving and read her the riot act until Rosalyn felt so guilty she'd gone back in her room. She had no reason to be angry with Noah—he'd done his job and stopped bad things from happening at the celebration.

Rosalyn felt a bit like a spoiled child denied candy. She wanted to go to him, to be with him again, but her pride and temper had gotten in the way. She'd only hurt herself in the end.

With a sigh, she hung up the towel beside the sink and thought about how she'd be able to see Noah before tonight. She didn't want to wait for dark—she wanted to set eyes on him now.

As if she'd conjured him from her imagination, Noah appeared at the back door, Whiskers at his feet. Rosalyn knew in a moment that something was wrong. His eyes brimmed with anger, frustration and need. Her first response was to throw her arms around him.

So she did.

Hard, warm arms wrapped around her, pulling her close until they were touching from head to toe. His whiskers scuffed against her cheek but she didn't care. His embrace was like coming home. She felt safe and treasured and perhaps loved. They'd come to know each other's bodies intimately but had work to do before they knew each other's hearts and minds. Rosalyn was afraid that once he knew her story, the whole story, he might change his mind about being with her.

She had to take a chance if she wanted more than midnight visits to heaven.

"I need to talk to you," she blurted before she lost her nerve. Whiskers meowed her approval.

Noah leaned back and met her gaze. "Me too."

"Outside with you." Rosalyn shooed the cat out the door, then walked over to peek through the door to the dining area. "Elsa's gone to gossip with her friends. Come to my room."

"Are you sure? I don't want her chasing me with a rolling pin."

Rosalyn laughed. "I promise to protect you. Please, I have some things I need to tell you."

Noah enfolded her hand in his. "Lead on, sweetheart."

Rosalyn's palms grew moist as they walked upstairs to her room. By the time they reached the door, she'd almost turned around four times. When she crossed the threshold, she realized the tiny room would make keeping her distance while she talked very difficult. Noah filled the space with his wide shoulders and long, lanky frame.

"Nice room. Elsa's treating you well." He sat on the edge of the bed and put his elbows on his knees.

Rosalyn chose the floor since the bed might get her off the subject of what she needed to tell him. As it was, she was having a hard time controlling the urge to kiss him. Now wasn't the time to kiss though.

"My daddy used to hit my mama all the time. He'd blacken her eyes a couple times a week, sometimes he'd even break a bone or two." The memory of the sound of his fists hitting flesh had haunted many of her nightmares. "He left me alone though. Maybe because I was too small and not enough sport, or maybe because my mama always came between him and me. Either way, my daddy was not a good man."

Noah focused completely on her, his brown eyes encouraging her to go on. She took a deep breath and prepared herself to rip the bandage off an old wound.

"One night, I must've done something that caught his attention because he hauled off and walloped me. My mother tried to come between us, but he just pushed her off. I was barely conscious at that point, and I'd lost half my baby teeth in that one smack." She closed her eyes against the memory of blood filling her mouth. "He picked me up and I remember dangling off the floor and seeing him through red. I think he must've had me by the neck. The next thing I knew, a gun went off. It was really loud in our little shack. My father dropped like a stone and so did I."

Rosalyn took a moment to catch her breath and try to swallow the tears that fell behind her eyes. Noah took a hand into his, silently urging her to continue.

"The town hung my mother before dawn and made me watch. I thought for sure they'd hang me too because I done something that made my daddy mad enough to try to kill me. I ran and hid where no one could find me."

"How old were you?" It was the first question he'd asked.

"Eight."

"Jesus Christ." He squeezed her hand. "No one bothered to help you?"

She shook her head. "They likely couldn't find me if they tried. I was real good at hiding. The first year I survived by eating rats I could catch and slops. When my cat sort of adopted me, I'd have meat a couple times a week from what she caught. I stole food from the mercantile and even clothes off a clothesline. I ain't proud of what I done, but I did it because I had to."

Rosalyn was afraid to look him in the eye. There was so much in her past that was rancid and bloody, the true bowels of humankind.

"I don't have what you call good family and maybe someday I'll take after my daddy or my mama. I could beat and murder folks any time now." She finally got the courage up to look him

149

in the eye, prepared to run, to return to the life she'd lived for ten years before a stubborn sheriff plucked her from the alley.

"Oh, honey, you aren't your parents. You're someone special, a survivor who has absolutely nothing to be ashamed of. Did you think I'd reject you because of what your parents did?"

"Yes," she blurted. "This entire town treats me like horse shit they want to scrape off their shoes. Why should you be any different?"

He cupped her face and kissed her so softly, she barely felt it. "Because I love you."

Because I love you.

She'd waited so long to hear someone, anyone, say that to her. Her mother had been affectionate to a point but never told her daughter she loved her. Although she shouldn't believe him, Rosalyn's heart grabbed hold of those words and hugged them tightly.

"Are you sure?" She could've kicked herself for asking, but she had to know.

Noah smiled, a sad, bittersweet smile that plucked her heart strings. "Positive. I was going to talk to you about something else but it can wait until tomorrow." He tucked her hair behind her ears. "Now why don't you lie beside me and I'll tell you my story."

Rosalyn had hoped he'd tell her something about himself too, but she didn't want to ask. Folks would either talk or they wouldn't. Forcing them to talk was always a bad idea. They settled on the bed with their backs resting against the wall. Noah put his arm around her shoulders and Rosalyn snuggled into his warm body.

"Your sins, sweet Rosalyn, are nothing compared to what I've done to survive. My mother was a cook on a ranch with about a dozen hands, but half her job was servicing the man who owned the ranch, Owen Hoffman. He'd come into our room whenever he felt like it and make her do whatever he wanted her to." He sounded so bitter, Rosalyn almost had to look to make sure it was Noah talking. "It could be three o'clock in the morning and he'd drag her out of bed."

He leaned over and put his nose in her hair, inhaling deeply before continuing.

"My mother died when I was twelve and I think she willed herself to die because she couldn't live like that anymore. That first night, I found out Hoffman expected me to take over where my mother had left off." Noah paused and Rosalyn took a moment to absorb what he meant.

She put her hand on his chest, feeling the rapid beat of his heart beneath her fingers.

"I wasn't as easy as she was, but as it turned out, the more I struggled, the more he liked it." He swallowed and sucked in a shaky breath. "I gave in to survive. I gave in for two years until a bounty hunter and his prisoner shot and killed Hoffman, setting me free. Turns out the outlaw and the bounty hunter had gotten married and wanted me to come work at their ranch. Until I met Nicky and Tyler Calhoun, I never knew life could be enjoyed and not just endured." He blew out a shaky breath and Rosalyn felt the rest of his body trembling beneath the raw emotions she heard in his voice.

She rolled over and tucked her head beneath his chin. As her arm wrapped around his chest, he squeezed her shoulder. Something wet landed on her hair and she wished she could take his pain away. Lord above, she knew for certain her heart had been completely and utterly given to him.

It was as if God had reached down and pointed the way to Chancetown for Noah. Someone or something had certainly guided his steps to hers.

"Do you want me to go?" His voice was husky with emotion and need.

"No, never." She kissed his neck. "I want you to make love to me."

"Are you sure?"

"I've never been more sure of anything in my life, Sheriff." She pulled his face to hers and met his lips in a fiery kiss that threatened to scald.

They exchanged long, soul-filled kisses with hot, wet tongues and nibbling teeth. She ended up lying on top of him, teasing him with butterfly kisses and slow licks across his full lips. Rosalyn tangled her fingers in his soft hair, loving the way it felt, loving him.

Noah kept repeating her name over and over, as if he couldn't believe she was there in his arms, that she was truly his. Rosalyn intended on showing him.

She skimmed her fingers along his buttons, then undid them one by one. He watched her with his shining brown eyes, ancient pain reflected in them. Rosalyn's heart beat a heavy, steady rhythm for him, for them, for love.

"Love me, Rosalyn," he whispered.

"I do."

Within moments, they'd shed their clothes and lay down side by side, their bodies within a hairsbreadth of touching. She traced each scar, each line on his skin. He shivered beneath her touch, closing his eyes. Noah had seemed so big, so strong to her, never afraid. Beneath that sheriff's badge lay a man who needed to be healed as much as she did.

Rosalyn leaned forward and kissed his eyelids, his cheeks, his nose, then finally his lips. Soft, warm and pliable, his mouth joined with hers. Unhurried, as if they had the rest of their lives, they kissed so many times Rosalyn lost count.

Slow kisses that sent shafts of desire all the way down her skin to land between her legs were followed by long kisses that made her dizzy. Her pussy came to life, knowing that she would join with him, but without the ravenous hunger she always felt.

This time it was about becoming one, and her heart and soul, not her body, led the way.

Rosalyn moved closer, raising her leg and nestling his cock against her. With her hand guiding him, he slid into her wetness, filling her, completing her. Sweet, sweet heaven.

Noah opened his eyes and stared into hers as they danced the eternal dance together. He cupped her breast and pressed his mouth to hers. Their tongues dueled in unison to their movements below. What began as a slow dance of love quickly picked up speed.

Rosalyn's blood rushed through her, pounding in her ears and between her legs. He thrust in and out, touching her womb, touching her heart. She moved with him, meeting his body, feeling the threat of her own release.

She scratched at his back, tangling her tongue with his. The bed squeaked beneath them, echoing the rhythm of their loving.

She lifted her leg high, allowing him to go deeper. He gasped as he sank to the hilt. Rosalyn's body shook with the love she had for the man who was now as deep within her as he could be, joined with her as one. She threw her head back and groaned.

"Oh God, Noah." A tear squeezed from her eye and rolled toward her nose. "I love you."

His hand gripped her knee and he pushed within her, pulling her closer and closer to the precipice of pleasure.

"Love you," he gasped as his body spasmed within her, spilling his seed.

Rosalyn dove over the cliff with him, the orgasm rolling through her like thunder, stealing her breath. She sought his lips blindly, unable to do more than feel the purest wave of love in her life.

Their lips met and sealed their union, forever.

Chapter Eleven

Noah's body still tingled from their lovemaking while his heart beat a steady rhythm of its own. He didn't remember feeling so free before. Telling Rosalyn his deepest, darkest secret was the hardest thing he'd ever done. Many women would have turned away or shunned him because of his choice. It had been a choice. He could have run away or said no—either option would have likely resulted in his death.

Instead, Noah had taken the "easy" road, although nothing about what he'd been through those two years had been easy. The experience had peppered his dreams, his nightmares for the last ten years. Perhaps now his soul could be more at peace with what he'd lived through.

Working as sheriff of Chancetown allowed him the opportunity to save himself by helping others. He couldn't think of a better way to spend his life, provided Rosalyn stood at his side.

They waited in the kitchen for Elsa, sipping coffee and thinking. He knew Rosalyn was working through her own thoughts about what they'd said and done. Every few minutes she looked up at him with a shy smile.

Elsa burst into the kitchen with a fierce frown. "Do you know how hard it was to keep a straight face while I could hear the two of you acting like rabbits upstairs?"

Rosalyn's cheeks blushed bright red and Noah resisted the urge to slap his forehead. Elsa helped that out by smacking him on the back of the head.

"I told you Rosie was a good girl."

"I'm sorry, Elsa, it's my fault. She—"

Rosalyn smacked him on the shoulder. "Don't say another word." Rosalyn's frown was as scary as Elsa's. "What I do is my own decision and no one else's. Don't you dare make excuses for me."

Elsa, the leader of the madhouse, smiled. "I'm glad to hear you stand up for yourself."

"I think me and Noah might get hitched and I don't think you should buy a horse without riding it," Rosalyn announced.

Noah almost choked to death on his mouthful of coffee. Jesus Christ on crutches. What the hell had she just said?

"I think you did the right thing," Elsa agreed.

This time Noah had a coughing fit that brought tears to his eyes. Elsa slapped him on the back repeatedly until he growled at her. She stepped back with both hands up in surrender.

"Just trying to save your life, Sheriff." She scowled. "No need to bite the hand that helps you."

Noah finally got his breath back. "You two are going to kill me."

Rosalyn laughed and kissed his cheek. "I don't think so. You just have to get used to ladies who speak their mind. About lots of things." She waggled her eyebrows.

Elsa burst out laughing as Noah's mouth dropped open. He'd never met two females who talked about sex so freely. Not that it was a bad thing, but a bit shocking.

And arousing.

Before his mind took him down a path he wasn't ready to follow, he mentally slapped himself to focus. He'd just spent an hour in bed with Rosalyn for pity's sake. The fact that Elsa knew that made him squirm. He shook his head to dispel the discomfort and tried to focus.

"I need to talk to both of you and Marina about something I found out today. Do you have time to go over to the saloon for a while?"

Elsa nodded. "It'll be another hour before the supper folks come. Let's go."

The three of them walked to the saloon in silence. Rosalyn tucked her hand in his and her small fingers curled around his. Elsa clomped along in front of them. The saloon wasn't busy at four in the afternoon during the week. Marina sat at the end of the bar with her chin in her hand.

She stood when they walked in, her eyes scanning Noah's. She murmured something to the bartender and waited for them.

"I don't expect you're here to say howdy." Marina's brows drew together.

"Do you have a private room we can talk in?" Noah asked quietly.

"In the back. Come on." She gestured for them to follow her.

Marina led them through a door in the corner into a private room with a table and four chairs. A private poker room if Noah wasn't mistaken. She must have some high rollers come in on occasion.

Elsa shut the door behind them and they all sat facing each other. "This is your dance, Sheriff. Get on with the music."

Noah thought about all that he'd learned that day and hoped talking it over with his friends would help him decide what to do.

"I went and talked to Johnny Boyton today. I found out that he had a deal with Shep Seeger and his cousin, Mayor Dickinson, to split money from the sale of sheep."

He let that sink in. It took about three beats before their reactions hit.

"What sheep? Seeger doesn't have any sheep." Elsa leaned forward, her expression suspicious.

"Apparently the herds from each and every sheepherder who's tried to settle in Chancetown." The idea of them stealing the lives of four men and now trying to snatch Finley's fueled Noah's anger again. "Those bastards don't want sheep because of the amount of grass they eat, so instead of putting up fences, they did everything they could to destroy these men."

Marina looked disappointed. "Johnny helped them?"

Noah covered her hand with his. "I know he's your friend, but he admitted it to me, Marina. Flat out told me that he looked the other way while they ran those men to the ground and took everything from them." His voice shook with fury. "I can't let them do the same thing to Finley. I can't."

Marina pulled her hand away. "Johnny's a good man, Noah. No matter what he's done, deep down, he's a good man."

"I'm not sure if I believe that as much as you do, but that's not important right now. He's hiding out on that farm. I need to put together a plan to stop Seeger and Dickinson. I thought maybe the three of you might help. I'm going to be honest with you, it isn't going to be fun, and it might be dangerous and deadly."

Rosalyn looked furious. "I'll help you. Seeger is one of the men who hung my mother. He's done taking from other people." She slammed her fist into the table. "Let's kill him."

Noah cupped her chin. "We don't want revenge, sweetheart. We want to put him and Dickinson in prison so they pay for what they've done."

"Killing is a pretty equal payment for what they done." Rosalyn's violet eyes sparked.

"I think Noah's right, Rosie." Elsa smiled without any humor. "Better to humiliate those sons of bitches in court and put them in a tiny dirty cell for the rest of their lives." She sounded like a bloodthirsty pirate.

"I have a question." Marina met Noah's gaze. "Why us? Why aren't you talking to some men in town?"

Noah had to think about the answer because up until that point, he hadn't even considered the people he chose to confide in were all women.

"I've seen some bad things in my life, most of them by men. My adopted mother is the strongest person I've ever met. She is strong, smart and the fastest draw in Wyoming. There are a lot of strong women in her family, the Malloys. Somewhere in the last ten years, the strength of women has equaled the strength of men in my mind."

Elsa and Marina both nodded.

Rosalyn stared at him as if he'd grown a second head. "Your mother carries a gun?"

"Yes and she wears britches too."

Elsa whistled. "I think I'm going to like her. A lot."

A pang of homesickness hit Noah and he had to push it away. It would be a dream come true to have Nicky and Tyler there, but this time he couldn't count on them to tell him what to do. He needed to make those decisions for himself.

"Will you help me? You don't have to and I won't force you to. I want this to be your decision."

Each of his friends all agreed to help do what they could, regardless of the consequences. He hadn't expected to find three people he trusted as much as his family, but he had. He took Rosalyn's hand in his. Touching her brought him back to the situation.

"Here's what I want to do. First, I'm going to talk to Finley and let him know what's going on, then get his agreement to help. In the meantime, I'm going to wire for a U.S. Marshal to come to Chancetown. We're going to set a trap." Noah had an idea of how to trap Seeger, but the trick was getting Dickinson too.

That's where his friends would come in.

"You three are going to help me trap Dickinson while Finley and I trap Seeger." He looked around at their faces. Determination met his gaze.

"Just tell us what we need to do. I never liked that weasel Dickinson anyway." Elsa flapped her hand. "He doesn't like peach pie. Who doesn't like peach pie?"

Her rancor broke the tension in the room and everyone chuckled a bit.

"Let's get those bastards." Rosalyn squeezed his hand. "Lead the way, Sheriff."

ଐ

Noah walked back to the jail from the telegraph office. He'd known the name of the marshal he needed to contact and was able to get the telegram sent and make it cryptic enough that most folks wouldn't understand it. He hoped Mark Jackman would come as soon as he could. In the meantime, he'd have to walk the line between being the sheriff and keeping himself and his friends alive.

As Noah approached the jail, he saw Finley waiting for him in the shadows next to the building. Noah had a feeling that something else had happened since the last time they'd spoken. He nodded at the sheep rancher and stepped inside, anticipating the big man would follow.

The inside of the jail wasn't as hot, and Noah took off his hat and fanned his face to cool off the late spring heat. Within moments, the door opened and Finley ducked in. Noah noticed a smear of dark red on the other man's neck. It sure looked like blood.

"Finley." Noah sat down heavily at the desk, the weight of the day like a rock on his shoulders.

"Sheriff, what's happening? I find twenty of my sheep dead this morning. They sheared them and slit their throats. The wool is gone and what's left of the animals was half-eaten by the damn coyotes." Finley shook, his pupils dilated. The man was near his breaking point.

Noah realized Finley was in shock. He stood and led the other man to the chair beside the desk. The wood creaked beneath his weight. The smell of sweat and fear surrounded him. Noah grabbed the pitcher of water on the small table.

"Cup your hands."

Finley held out shaking hands and Noah poured some water onto the calloused palms.

"Put some water on your face and take some deep breaths."

Finley slowly rubbed the cool liquid on his forehead and cheeks. Noah filled the tin cup on the desk, figuring any leftover coffee in the bottom wouldn't be noticeable to the other man. Nicky had taught Noah how to treat wounds and medical problems, like shock. It had helped more than once out on the range when a cowboy needed attention.

Noah handed him a cup, and Finley stared down into its depths. After about five minutes, he stopped trembling. Noah kept his tongue in check until he figured the other man was ready to talk. It wouldn't be much longer.

"My sheep are innocent. They don't deserve this." Finley looked up at Noah with anger in his light blue eyes.

"I agree with you, Finley. I'm working on stopping it. It's going to be dangerous and I need to know you're not going to pack up and run." Noah squatted down so they were eye to eye.

"What is more dangerous than what I am doing right now? Each day I wake up and wonder how many sheep I will have, or if I will wake up." Finley nodded. "I will do whatever you need me to do."

$\wp$

The moon streamed through the open window as the blue curtains fluttered in the sweet evening breeze. Rosalyn snuggled up next to Noah and kissed his chest. Life had never been so wonderful for her. She had a man who loved her, true friends, and more than that, a future. She closed her eyes and sighed, drifting off with the man she loved beneath her cheek.

The next thing she knew, she was gasping for air as her eyes stung and she smelled smoke. Noah was no longer in the bed with her.

"Noah?" She coughed and sat up, her head swimming. Everything seemed unfocused and dark.

Noah appeared in a blur on the floor beside the bed. "The jail's on fire," he shouted, then coughed like an invalid. "We need to get out of here as soon as possible."

Rosalyn could hardly see him through the smoke. It must've been daylight because patches of light poked through the clouds around them. It was early though, probably near dawn. Orange flames licked the window, leaving black splotches behind.

"We have to go down the stairs." He yanked the blanket off the bed. "Wrap this around you."

Rosalyn tried to stand, but dizziness landed her back on the bed. Noah wrapped the blanket around her head, then dumped water from the pitcher on her. She gasped at the cold.

"Cover your mouth, sweetheart. I don't know if this is going to work, but we've got to get out of here." He kissed her hard. "I love you."

Rosalyn tried to speak but her throat burned too badly.

"Ready?" Noah helped her to her feet.

She nodded. He dumped the rest of the water on his head and they started toward the door. The floor felt heated and small hisses of smoke escaped through the floorboards. Rosalyn heard cracks and pops as the building burned beneath them and around them. She'd never felt so scared in her life.

Noah put his hand on the door and pulled back quickly. "It's warm, but not hot. There's no other way out, Rosie, we've got to."

Rosie.

He'd never called her that before, and her heart hiccupped when he did. Elsa had started calling her that, but Noah doing it was more than sweet, it was perfect. Rosalyn could have kicked her own ass for turning into a mushy fool when they were fighting for their lives. Still, she snatched the small moment and held onto it tight.

Noah opened the door and a rush of heat made her eyelashes curl. She buried her head against his shoulder and hung on. They walked out onto the stairs and she peered over his shoulder. Black smoke curled up with sparks of orange and red. It looked like the bowels of hell and they had to get through it to survive.

He grabbed her hand and started down one step at a time. Rosalyn kept the blanket across her mouth and nose, breathing in small snatches of wet wool. By the time they were halfway down, the heat was intense, the sound of the fire like a roaring monster below. Fear raced through her, fear she'd lose her own life or even worse, she'd lose Noah.

She gripped Noah's hand, her nails digging into his skin. When they were almost at the bottom, he slipped. Rosalyn kept hold of his hand, hanging on with every ounce of her strength, nearly wrenching her arm from the socket. He regained his footing and glanced at her through the smoke, mouthing "thank you". She told him with her eyes that she loved him, and amazingly enough, he seemed to understand.

When they reached the foot of the stairs, the crackling of the fire was deafening. Rosalyn could hardly see the door through the smoke and flames. They started forward and something pushed at her back, then the floor rushed up to meet her.

"Rosie! Oh my God." Noah kicked the beam off her, then used the wet blanket to beat the flames licking at her. At the same time he beat back his panic. He hadn't expected the building to collapse so quickly and certainly not on top of her. She was *not* dead—she couldn't be.

Rosalyn was alive, just had the wind knocked out of her. Noah would not accept she was anything but unconscious. The fire around them was hot enough to make his skin feel like it was already sizzling. His lungs burned so badly, he tried to hold his breath until he felt dizzy. When he finally dragged in a breath, he coughed so hard, he got a stitch in his side. He had to get out of there fast.

Noah wrapped her in the blanket and dragged her across the floor on his knees. He saw the door but it seemed to be a million miles away. When the flames got closer, Noah crawled faster. His knees screamed in agony from the heat of the wood and the splinters embedding themselves in his skin. The palm of his left hand blistered and popped but he ignored the pain. He would not die in a fire, nor would he let the woman he loved die because of him.

A bright shaft of light stung his eyes, and a gust of wind fanned the flames around him.

"Noah?"

He was imagining things, he had to be. The voice had sounded exactly like his father, Tyler.

"Where are you, boy?"

Noah coughed and sucked in too much smoke again. He choked and continued crawling, sure he was about to die. Rosalyn, however, had to live, no matter what. He'd get her out of that damn building even if he was burning like a torch. Noah had set out to help her, now he needed to save her life.

When he was ten feet from the door, a pair of boots stepped up beside him. It took too much effort to look up, so he kept on crawling, towing Rosalyn behind him.

"Her feet are smoking, Noah."

The boots stepped away and Noah finally got a breath of fresh air from the open door. He was so close. Just another five feet until they were free.

The boots were back and the man wearing them squatted beside him. "Noah, let me help you."

Noah looked up into the blue eyes of his adopted father, Tyler Calhoun. A bit of gray mixed with the black hair around the temples and some wrinkles beside his ice blue eyes were the only changes in the last ten years. He was still as big, hard and fierce as ever.

On any other day, Noah would be surprised to see him. However, the day seemed to be in another world than the usual, which meant anything could happen. Since he hadn't contacted his parents in a long time, they didn't know where he was therefore he must be imagining things. It didn't matter, he'd take help from wherever he could get it, even mirages.

"Got...to...get...her...out. Love...her...Pa." Noah made it to the door and out onto the sidewalk.

He kept going, dragging Rosalyn behind him until they were both out onto the hard-packed dirt in the street. He lay on his back, sucking in gulps of air until he felt even more lightheaded. Noah heard the bells of the fire brigade and people shouting. Then his father appeared above him again, shaking his head.

"Trouble seems to follow us, doesn't it?" He glanced at Rosalyn. "This your lady?"

"Rosalyn," Noah whispered.

When his mother, Nicky, floated into his vision, he knew he was dying. A frown marred the peach-colored freckled face, while green eyes danced with concern. Her reddish brown hair swung from a long braid beneath her flat-brimmed hat.

"Looks like we got here just in time."

Noah tried to laugh but it was more of a squeak. He was either dying or he'd lost his mind. Why would his parents be there? Hell, they didn't know where he was—he'd deliberately kept it that way.

Nicky cupped his cheek and the feel of her familiar hand brought a tear to his eye. God how he missed her.

"We'll take care of you and your lady. Don't worry."

He shut his eyes and gave into the blackness closing around him.

℘

Cool water trickled over his face, pulling him from the pit that had swallowed him. He blinked and focused on the face above his. After a minute, he realized he was looking at his mother.

"Ma?"

Nicky frowned fiercely but he could see relief in her eyes. "Welcome back."

Noah looked around at an unfamiliar room. He tried to sit up and a coughing fit hit. As he struggled for breath, she rubbed his back until the spasms passed. After he was able to breathe again, he recognized the room as the upstairs of the saloon, if he wasn't mistaken. He heard voices, glasses clinking and laughter somewhere in the building.

"Where's Rosalyn?" His scratchy voice didn't even sound like him.

"She's over at the restaurant with a woman named Elsa." Tyler stepped into his line of vision. "Tough little thing, almost knocked me on my ass."

"Is she okay?" Noah wanted to shake them for keeping him waiting.

"I'm not sure." Nicky took his hand in hers. "The doctor refused to see her. He treated you but that's because apparently you're the sheriff."

"The sheriff thing was a surprise." Tyler's blue gaze searched Noah's for answers. "I'd be mighty curious to hear about it."

"I'll tell you the whole story when I can take a breath without coughing. Water." He pointed to the pitcher.

Nicky brought him a cup of water and he drank it in small sips, savoring the cool liquid on his burning throat. His guts churned with anger for the way Rosalyn was still being treated. That damn doctor was about to realize that he couldn't treat people like dogs and get away with it.

Not while Sheriff Noah Calhoun was on the job.

He sat up and swung his legs to the side of the bed. A wave of dizziness made him grip the covers to stay upright.

"Where the hell are you going?" Tyler frowned, all six foot two of him.

Noah might have backed down a few years ago, but not now.

"I'm going to make that fucking doctor treat her or throw the bastard in jail." He stood slowly, sucking in a breath at the pain in every square inch of his body.

"The doctor said you need to stay in bed for a couple of days," Nicky observed. "I don't think you're going to listen, are you?"

"Not to one word that idiot said." He met her gaze. "This town treats Rosalyn so badly it makes me—"

"I got that already." She touched his arm. "We'll do what you want us to, but remember, you're not alone. Your family is here."

His family. They'd proved themselves countless times to be his family, that they loved and supported him. Noah had kept a part of himself tucked away from the Calhouns and Malloys. He owed them an apology but that would have to wait. Now he needed to focus on Rosalyn and making sure she was okay.

Noah hugged his mother quickly, surprised to feel a tremor run through her. Nicky had always been the toughest, roughest woman he'd ever known, and the most loving. Never gave an inch, never backed down.

"You might want to wash." She touched his cheek and brought back a blackened hand.

Tyler snorted and shook his head. "Wouldn't do any good for your lady to see you looking like a raccoon."

Noah hobbled over to the basin and stared at the reflection in the mirror above the bureau. His hair was as black as his face, only the whites of his eyes were visible. His clothes were covered with small holes and tears. He couldn't even begin to start listing all the places that hurt because the one that hurt the most was his heart.

He had to get to Rosalyn.

Chapter Twelve

Rosalyn heard voices around her. They were mumbling or maybe she just couldn't hear what they said. Her head hurt and the more she tried to listen, the worse the pain got. So she stopped trying. Instead, she thought about Noah, then she remembered the fire.

Her heart thumped as she realized he could be dead. She could be lying here and the sounds she heard could be people getting his body ready for burial. Rosalyn cried out soundlessly in protest. Noah could not be dead. Not when she'd just found him. God couldn't be that cruel.

The way she figured it, He owed her and she aimed to collect by getting to keep Noah Calhoun from here on out. Rosalyn forced her eyes open and had trouble seeing anything. Her eyes stung like somebody had rubbed salt in them. It was all blurry at first, then she was able to distinguish the window in her room. She was at Elsa's in her own bed. The voices belonged to Elsa and Marina.

"Rosie?" Elsa loomed over her. "You're awake. Thank Mary and all her good nature."

Marina appeared with a small smile. "You had us worried there for a while. After the doctor—I mean, we did the best we could but you sucked in a lot of smoke."

It hurt to breathe so Rosalyn sucked in little bits of air at a time.

"N-N-Noah?" she managed to squeak out.

"He's over at the saloon in one of the upstairs rooms." Marina patted her hand. "His parents arrived yesterday during the fire. He was right about his mama. She's a fierce woman and that husband of hers..."

Elsa harrumphed. "He's as big as a brick wall, that ex-bounty hunter. I ain't afraid of him."

Noah's parents were there? How had that happened? Had he telegraphed them? Rosalyn's body felt like she'd been trampled by horses and each deep breath was agony.

"You need to sleep, honey." Elsa patted her cheek. "Don't you worry about a thing now. You and Noah survived. The jail didn't but nobody got killed and that's what's important."

Rosalyn didn't care about the jail, she just wanted to see Noah, to touch him and make sure he was okay. She pleaded with her eyes because talking made her throat feel as if she'd swallowed the fire.

"I'll go check on him, okay?" Marina offered.

Rosalyn nodded, grateful again for finding friends who would help her. She'd lived so long all alone, the bounty of having a family, even if they weren't really related, was more than she'd ever imagined.

જી

Noah stumbled into the doctor's office and gripped the doorframe. Dr. Ramsey glanced up in surprise from his chair next to the window. A book dropped from his lap as he stood.

"Sheriff Calhoun, what are you doing out of bed? I told your parents—"

"You refused to treat Rosalyn Benedict," Noah ground out.

"Well, yes, I see paying patients and that girl is nothing but street trash, no matter what you think, without two pennies to rub together." Dr. Ramsey brought himself up to his full height of five foot six and stuck his nose so high in the air, Noah could see clear up to his walnut-sized brain.

"Rosalyn is my future wife, Doc. Now I suggest unless you want to be arrested and spend a few days locked in Elsa's cellar, that you get your sorry ass over there and treat her wounds." Noah pulled the gun from the holster his father had had to help him put on. He cocked the pistol and aimed it at the doctor. "Now."

Doctor Ramsey glanced between Noah and his parents behind him and fear replaced the superiority in his beady eyes. No doubt Nicky and Tyler stood with their legs spread, arms crossed or better yet, hovering over their own pistols. Noah would say one thing for his family, they knew how to be menacing.

"Fine then, but I expect to be paid or I'll take it up with the mayor." He stepped over to the corner and picked up his medical bag.

A gold coin flew across the room and slapped the doctor in the chest. He squealed and jumped a foot in the air. Noah had to bite his lip to stifle the chuckle at the man's reaction.

"There's your money, you windbag. Now get your ass over to Elsa's," Tyler growled from behind Noah.

The doctor picked up the twenty-dollar gold piece and tucked it in his pocket. Noah's opinion of the greed that ran rampant in the town was confirmed again. Give a man enough money and he'd sell his soul for more.

They headed over to Elsa's as quickly as Noah could walk. Halfway there, his mother took his arm in hers and half-supported him. He couldn't even say thank you, he was so afraid he'd fall on his face if he tried.

When they arrived, Marina was just walking outside. She smiled when she saw Noah, then frowned after realizing Nicky was supporting him. Her dark eyes clouded with concern.

"You shouldn't be out of bed, Noah," Marina admonished.

"Marina, these are my parents, Nicky and Tyler Calhoun. This is Marina Fuerte, she owns the saloon." Noah's vision started to gray and suddenly he was scooped up in his father's arms.

Tears blurred his eyes at being held by the very man he wanted to be. Tyler Calhoun had given him a new life and Noah loved him fiercely.

"Where is she?" Tyler barked at Marina.

Nicky frowned at her husband. "Nice to meet you, Marina. Could you tell us where Rosalyn is?"

Marina led the group of them inside and up the stairs, with Doctor Ramsey bringing up the rear. Noah floated in and out of consciousness as Tyler carried him, seemingly without effort, up an entire flight of stairs. When they made it to Rosalyn's bedroom, Tyler laid Noah down on the bed as gently as he would have a babe.

Rosalyn's scent surrounded him and Noah groped for her hand. She was warm and alive beside him. Thank God. She coughed and Noah turned to look at her, shocked by how red and blistered her face was, but her eyes were open and she was alive.

He cupped her chin. "I love you, Rosie."

Tears spilled down her face and she pressed her forehead to his. Even though he felt half-dead, just being near her gave him a surge of life, of hope.

"Am I to treat her or not?" Doctor Ramsey interjected.

"Hold your water, fool. Can't you see they're talking?" Tyler snapped.

Noah closed his eyes for a moment, grateful to have Rosalyn beside him again, thankful her heart still beat beside his.

"I brought the doctor, sweetheart. He's going to treat your burns and make sure you're okay." He kissed the tip of her nose, the only place that didn't look like it was burned.

She mouthed "okay" and squeezed his hand.

Noah looked up at his father. "I need to move so the doc can get to her."

Tyler scooped him up again and brought him to the rocking chair in the corner. His father knelt down and put his hand on Noah's knee, his blue gaze serious.

"Being a lawman isn't an easy job. My pa did it until he died doing it. I'm right proud of you, son." A suspicious gleam appeared in his father's eyes, but he stood before Noah could get a good look.

His mother came to stand beside him, her hand resting on his shoulder with Tyler on the other side. A roomful of folks who cared about him seemed like paradise on earth.

If only someone hadn't just tried to kill him and Rosalyn, life would be about perfect.

೮ා

An hour later, the doctor left, his nose in the air again. Noah made a note to himself to find a new doctor for Chancetown. That one was obviously not a keeper. By then, Noah had drunk some coffee and eaten one of Elsa's biscuits. He felt much better and was able to walk over to the bed without help.

Marina and Elsa took his parents downstairs for a late breakfast, leaving Noah alone with Rosalyn.

He sat on the edge of the bed and took her bandaged hand in his. Her violet gaze stared at him with so many emotions, he drowned in their depths.

"We're a pair, aren't we? Bandaged, burned and smelling like we got stuck in the oven."

She smiled and squeezed his hand. "Love you." It was weak and so scratchy he barely heard it.

"I love you too, Rosie. You think you might see your way clear to marry me? After my hair grows back and the bandages come off?" His body shook with the thought that he'd just stepped off the cliff of safety and into the world of real life. No more drifting and trying to find the place where he belonged. He'd found it, right in the arms of the black-haired waif who chopped off her hair and dunked him in the trough.

Tears pooled in her eyes and she nodded slightly.

"Was that a yes?"

"Yes."

Although neither one of them could move or breathe easily, Noah stretched out next to her and tucked her under his arm. This is what he wanted each and every morning and night. Noah had finally come home. It was only after he could touch her that he was able to sleep.

Noah didn't leave Rosalyn's side until late afternoon. Being together had been a healing in and of itself. He walked down the stairs slowly, holding onto the wall for support. The smells of supper cooking, perhaps a stew, made his mouth water. They had barely eaten during the day and his stomach yowled.

He found his parents in the dining room, sitting by the window at a table drinking coffee. They both glanced up when he walked in, relief still evident on their faces.

"Where are the young'uns?" Noah asked as he sat down.

"Mama is watching them. Let me tell you, your brother Logan almost got a whooping for trying to sneak off with us." Nicky shook her head. "That boy is just like his father."

Tyler snorted. "Like hell, magpie."

Logan was eight and as full of fire and sass as his mother. The thought of the boy he'd known and the young man he'd become made Noah's heart skip a beat. He'd missed his sisters too, Rebecca and Frankie. Three years was a lifetime to a child. Regret coated his tongue and it took him a few minutes to be able to speak.

"I'm sorry I haven't contacted you in six months. I've been trying to find the place I belong—"

"You belong at home with us. We adopted you because we love you like a son, Noah." His mother's green eyes flashed with confusion and hurt.

"I know and for that, I will always be grateful. You both gave me life, like I was born on that fall day when I saw Pa riding toward me." Noah's throat got tight. "I love you both very much, but I had to leave. Working the ranch didn't give me everything I needed. Then when I screwed up and Hercules almost k-killed Pa..."

Nicky covered his hand with hers. "You didn't mean for any of that to happen. There's no blame here. He survived because of what you did for him out there on the range."

"Because you taught me what to do." His knowledge of how to treat wounds had literally saved him from making the biggest mistake of his life—causing his father's death.

"How did you become sheriff?" His father watched him with his never-miss-anything gaze.

"That's a long story and for that I need food. Is Elsa around?" Noah glanced toward the kitchen.

"She's feeding Mark Jackman back there." Nicky pointed.

"Marshal Jackman is here?" Noah was impressed the other man had gotten there within days of the telegram. It shouldn't impress him though—it was standard for the big marshal to move quickly and with deadly speed.

"That's why we're here." Tyler raised one ebony eyebrow.

Noah should have expected that. His father and Mark had known each other more than fifteen years and were as close as brothers.

Tyler continued. "Mark hightailed it to us when he got your telegram. Nearly rode his horse into the ground. We came here together about ten minutes after that."

"It wasn't ten minutes." Nicky frowned.

"Okay nine and a half. She couldn't get her guns strapped on fast enough." His father winked at his wife. "Nothing like a woman wearing iron that makes a man sit up and notice."

"Oh, I don't need to hear this." Noah rose and headed toward food. "I'm going to get some supper and then we can talk."

Mark Jackman was a blond version of Tyler Calhoun. Big, mean and bad enough to scare criminals into giving themselves up. He'd worked with the ex-bounty hunter some years back and they'd become friends. Mark had visited the Bounty ranch where the Calhouns lived over time and Noah had followed the lawman around like a puppy during those visits. He was another man Noah had hoped to emulate.

Perhaps it was then that being a lawman had settled in Noah's head and arriving in Chancetown was no accident. Someone or something must have guided him into town to not only find the woman of his heart, but become the man he was meant to be.

Mark stood and whistled as Noah walked in. "Damn, boy, you turned out almost as big as your pa. At the moment, you look like a burned piece of toast though." He stuck out his hand and pumped Noah's hard enough to knock him off balance. "Sorry about that, kid. Your folks told me about the jail fire. Damn bastards."

He picked up his plate and sat again. "Tell me what's going on here, Noah." His gaze had turned serious and alert.

"I've got to have some food first, then I'll tell all three of you the story. Just know that some money-grubbing bastards have been up to no good and I need to catch them and put their sorry asses in jail."

Elsa walked through the back door. "Glad you're not dead, Sheriff. I'd hate to break in another one after you worked out right good. You want some supper?"

"Yes, ma'am. Anything you've got. My stomach is yowling something fierce." Noah eyed the biscuit Mark was currently eating and wondered if he could snatch the other off the marshal's plate before he noticed.

Mark shook his head, as if he'd sensed what Noah was planning. "Don't even think about touching my food, boy."

"No fighting, boys. I've got a plate in the warming oven for you." Elsa bustled over and used a towel to pull a heaping plate of ham, potatoes and biscuits from the oven.

"Elsa, if I didn't love Rosalyn, I'd marry you." He kissed her wrinkled cheek.

"Oh, get out of here before I take you up on that." She waved her hand in the air, but Noah swore he saw a touch of pink on her wrinkled cheeks. "I'll bring you some coffee out in the dining room. Marshal, why don't you head out there too. I'll bring a pot."

The two men walked into the dining room and settled at the table with Tyler and Nicky. Everyone spoke of nonsense while Noah shoveled the food into his yowling gullet. It tasted like ambrosia, sweet, salty and heavenly. He washed it down with three cups of coffee and followed up with a resounding belch.

Mark and Tyler laughed while Nicky frowned.

"Why do men think that burping and farting are something to crow about?" She gave each of them a quelling glance. "Next thing you'll be having a booger-flicking contest."

The three men howled with laughter while his mother tried to look as if it wasn't funny and failing miserably. Lord, Noah had missed the laughter and lightness he got from being around his family. He vowed to himself right then and there that no more than three months would go by without seeing them. Three years had been a lifetime.

"Now that your belly is obviously full, tell us what's going on." His mother had turned back into Nicky Calhoun, the former outlaw who had evaded the best bounty hunters for three years using only her cunning intelligence.

"It started ten years ago," Noah began. He recited the information he'd learned from Johnny Boyton, including the fact that the old sheriff had lined his pockets with money from the sheepherders who had been cheated and terrorized. Tyler remembered Boyton, but hadn't had more than a handful of dealings with him. Noah told them about how he'd gotten the job and been set up to either be a dirty sheriff or die in a ditch somewhere.

When he got to Rosalyn, he skimmed over the unusual parts of their courtship but included how badly the town treated her because of the sins of her parents. He also revealed that he loved her and had asked her to marry him.

Tyler grinned from ear to ear while his mother hugged him so tightly his ribs almost cracked.

Noah continued on to explain how he'd investigated both Seeger and Finley's claims of foul deeds and confirmed with the land office that Seeger had lied about land boundaries. With Johnny's information, he knew that Seeger had also lied about not being the cause of the sheep rancher's problems.

"Now the crooked bastards tried to burn me alive." Noah seethed with the knowledge they'd almost succeeded. He and Rosalyn had barely gotten out in time.

"Folks in town are talking about how the sheriff is at death's door. Had to be carried inside by some man, looking like he wouldn't make it a day." His father tapped the wooden table. "I think you can use that to set your trap."

His mind racing, Noah knew it was a great idea. "That's perfect. I already talked to Finley about setting up Dickinson and Seeger. We can get both of them at the same time with Mark listening." Noah coughed. "Elsa can fuel the rumor that I'm dying so they won't be expecting me."

"Sounds good. I love the idea of you coming back to life. You'll need to stay cooped up in here and away from the windows," Nicky offered while his father nodded.

Noah breathed a big sigh of relief at their approval. He had help and enough of it to catch the dirty bastards. Now he had to heal up and carefully plan what they needed to do.

"I'd say the old sheriff picked the right man for this job," Mark mused. "My guess is you've already got a plan and needed my help to make it work."

"Exactly." Noah's determination to clean up Chancetown finally had a fighting chance. "Will you help me?"

"Are you kidding? Dirty government, crooked sheriffs, murder and mayhem? What's not to love about it?" Mark laughed and pounded the table with his fist. "When do we start? I'm ready for some fun."

"Let's give them two weeks to stew in their own juices and wonder what's going to happen to me. Then they'll be expecting my funeral instead of theirs." Noah rubbed his forehead. "Now I just need to convince Rosalyn to keep her nose out of it."

He knew it wouldn't be an easy task. Rosalyn was a strong woman who'd taken care of herself for so long she wasn't used to waiting for something to happen. Noah respected her for that, but he wasn't about to risk her life because she was stubborn.

It would be a tricky job to convince her to stay put. However, Noah couldn't do what he needed to unless he knew she was safe. He'd almost lost her once and couldn't bear to think about it again.

Chapter Thirteen

It took almost two weeks for Rosalyn to heal enough to do her normal chores. The burns itched as they healed and sometimes she had trouble catching her breath. However, she was alive and incredibly grateful to be so, even more grateful that Noah had survived too. Elsa let Whiskers in to visit at least once a day. The cat's presence comforted Rosalyn when she felt alone and frustrated, which was a lot lately. She wasn't a good patient.

Noah's father scared the hell out of her. He was big enough to fill a room, and not just his physical size either. It was as if the room would never be big enough to hold the man. Noah's mother was a different story. She was outspoken, funny and dressed in britches with guns strapped to her hips.

Rosalyn adored Nicky.

They'd somehow made it a habit to have afternoon tea—which really meant milk or coffee—and cookies in Rosalyn's room. Those hour-long visits were something Rosalyn would treasure for a very long time. She could understand how Noah loved his mother so much. She was the backbone of the family.

Nicky told her all about her family, the Malloys. Rosalyn felt as if she knew each of them personally through the vivid descriptions. She laughed, cried and was enraptured by the folks who had raised Noah. Rosalyn now knew what it was that made Noah who he was—he was truly loved by these people.

It was hard for her to imagine living in a house with so much of everything—and she didn't mean things like furniture. What she remembered of her own house was darkness, and lots of it. Noah had shown her what it meant to be around people who cared what happened to you, but Noah's family took that one step further. To a place where Rosalyn now dearly wished to be.

As she listened to Nicky tell a story about Noah's little sister, Frankie, Rosalyn's breath hitched. Nicky stopped and scrutinized her.

"What's wrong?"

"Nothing, I'm feeling good. I ain't scratched once today. Tomorrow I can start working again. The doctor said so." She didn't mind the little white lie. No one had to know the doctor hadn't been back once.

Nicky's left eyebrow rose. "Somehow I get the feeling you're not telling me the whole truth, but every woman is entitled to her secrets."

Rosalyn just nodded, unable to respond. Noah had asked her to marry him and be a part of the family she could now see was like heaven on Earth. What stood between her and that paradise were two men intent on keeping their dirty money and secrets.

"We're going to stop them right?" Rosalyn blurted.

"You mean those two idiots, Seeger and Dickinson?"

"Yep. Sometimes I just want to ride over there and shoot them." Rosalyn seethed with rage over what they'd done.

"Me too," Nicky confessed. "Do you know how to fire a gun?"

"No, I ain't never held one either." Rosalyn sighed. "Don't have occasion to use one on the slops bucket."

Nicky chuckled. "Would you like me to teach you?"

"Is this a trick?" Rosalyn's heart leapt at the idea. Nicky was someone she truly wanted to be like. If the older woman was going to teach her to shoot, Rosalyn would be an eager pupil.

"No, no trick." Nicky squeezed her hand. "If you're up to it—"

Rosalyn threw back the quilt and climbed out of bed, searching for her blue dress, anxious to wear something besides a nightgown.

"I guess you're up to it," Nicky observed. "If you're looking for your dress, it was destroyed in the fire. Noah brought you something else to wear."

Nicky pointed to the hooks behind the door. Rosalyn walked over with her stomach quivering and her palms itching. Behind the door hung three dresses, each one a different shade of purple.

"Elsa helped him get the dresses since he can't be seen in town yet. He was very particular about it and made sure they matched your eyes, depending on your mood."

Rosalyn held the door for a moment, trying to regain the breath that had been knocked from her body. Noah had gifted her with much more than a few dresses. How had her life changed so much in a month? She blinked back a tear and picked the darkest dress, a rich shade of purple that reminded her of the sky before a twister hit.

She slipped it on over the chemise Elsa had given her. It was a perfect fit again. The soft cotton felt familiar and Rosalyn knew meeting Noah had changed the path of her life, her heart and her view on the world. She was, however, still the same person.

Rosalyn turned to Nicky with a grin. "When do we start the shooting lessons?"

They snuck down the back stairs to avoid any questions by the men. Nicky gathered a half dozen empty tin cans from the kitchen and put them in a sack. After checking her ammunition stores, they stepped outside. Elsa was outside beating a rug when they came out. She glanced at the two of them with a question in her eyes.

"Every woman needs to know how to shoot a gun." Nicky took Rosalyn's arm and headed off.

Elsa never said a word.

A bubble of happiness floated inside Rosalyn as she breathed in the warm early-summer air. She was a little stiff, but the walking felt wonderful. It had been some time since Rosalyn had been outside. She wasn't surprised to find how much she missed it. After all, she'd spent ten years of her life living outside all day, every day.

The sun peeped through the green leaves of the big oak trees as they headed for the open field. The day couldn't be more beautiful. She took a deep breath for the first time in weeks.

"I saw a fence back here with a small ravine behind it. It'll be perfect." Nicky pointed at a crooked wooden fence. "We'll set up the targets and get shooting."

Rosalyn had been excited to learn how to shoot, but now she felt a bit nervous. She could use a knife or a stick to defend herself. They were handy weapons anyone could use. A pistol was a different story altogether.

Nicky pulled the pistol from the left holster and handed it butt first to Rosalyn. She stared at the pearl handle, uncertain and annoyed with herself for feeling that way.

"Go on, take it. It won't bite, I promise." Nicky chuckled.

Rosalyn took the gun, surprised at how heavy it was. The smell of oil and gunpowder tickled her nose.

"Hold it like this with your thumb wrapped around this side and your fingers around the other." Nicky demonstrated with her other pistol. "Keep your index finger near the trigger, without touching it. These were modified to have a very easy trigger. Don't need you shooting me before we start."

After they both laughed, Rosalyn moved her hand around to grip the pistol as Nicky told her to.

"The key is to keep your elbow slightly bent. If you keep it stiff, the kickback will knock you on your ass." Nicky turned toward the tin cans on the fence. "Now, hold it out straight like this, keep your elbow bent."

Rosalyn held the gun out, pointing it at the cans, her arm shaking from the weight of the iron. How did Nicky hold it without difficulty?

"Don't worry, it gets easier. You build up your muscles to hold the weight, balancing it so your arms don't get sore." Nicky turned her body so she was angled to the left. "Protect yourself as best you can by keeping yourself at an angle. Nothing like a full chest target to tempt someone to kill you."

Rosalyn turned her body to match Nicky's, the bubble of excitement dancing in her stomach again.

"Now, the first target is the can on the far right. Close your left eye and sight down the center of the pistol at the can." Nicky's voice was low. "Steady your arm a bit."

A calm settled over Rosalyn as she stared at the tin can, focusing everything on the empty can of peaches. The gun still felt awkward in her hands, but it was beginning to feel like it belonged there.

"Now, slowly pull your finger back and when you're ready, squeeze the trigger. Don't jerk it or you'll end up on your ass wondering how you shot down that hawk." Nicky glanced at her. "Pretend that's Shep Seeger."

After an initial spurt of rage, a dead calm washed over Rosalyn as she stared at the can. Everything around her faded, including the twittering birds and buzzing insects. Her breath eased in and out and her heart beat a steady tattoo.

"Go on, Rosie. Shoot."

Rosalyn squeezed the trigger. The power of the bullet sent her stumbling backwards with a roar in her ears as the smell of the spent powder filled her nose. She coughed and wiped her eyes. Who knew shooting a gun could be so exciting?

"Did I get it?"

Nicky laughed. "No, but you did nick the fence."

Rosalyn whooped, a huge grin on her face. "Let's do it again."

"She's what?"

Noah looked out behind the restaurant and heard the far-off sounds of gunfire. Target shooting to be sure, and it was his mother and his woman?

"Did you say my mother was teaching Rosalyn how to shoot?" He turned back to Elsa, his stomach taking residence near his heart.

"That's what I said, Sheriff. Ain't nothing wrong with a woman knowing how to shoot a gun. Your ma is dang fast with those things too. *Whooeee*, she could give many a man a run for their money." Elsa grinned. "I like your ma a lot."

Noah shook his head and wondered if his life would ever be normal. He met his father's resigned gaze over the rim of the coffee mug.

"You've got to take it all, son. All or nothing with a woman like that."

Noah knew being married to the dark-haired waif would be nothing if not interesting. Protecting herself was important, but he hated to think she was learning to shoot because of the fire, because he hadn't kept her safe. He could and would protect her, even with his life. Rosalyn shouldn't need to know how to shoot.

Thirty minutes later, after Noah had nearly worn a hole in the floor, Rosalyn returned with Nicky. They blew into the kitchen with huge smiles on their faces and the scent of gunpowder around them. One look at Rosalyn's face and all of Noah's worries went away on a breeze. Her short black hair stuck up every which way and she had gunpowder on her nose. She'd never looked more alive or more beautiful.

He cupped her face and kissed her hard. "You need a set of pistols now?"

"Oh, I'd love some." She glanced at Nicky, her grin even wider. "That would be wonderful."

Noah laughed and hugged her close. The smell of outdoors, guns and woman washed over him. Lord he loved her.

Nicky patted her holsters. "Your lady is a natural. Within five minutes, she was taking down every one of those cans."

"I'm not surprised. Rosie is something special," Noah boasted, still trying to overcome the idea that his woman had learned how to shoot a pistol. From his mother.

"I love it. Don't know why I didn't do it before now." Rosalyn eyed Nicky's pistols with envy. "I understand now why every woman should learn how to shoot."

Tyler raised his eyes heavenward. "Magpie, it's a good thing I love you."

Nicky waggled her eyebrows. "You've got that backwards, bounty hunter."

Tyler swatted at his wife's backside. "You're gonna embarrass your son if you keep that up."

"He's seen worse." Nicky kissed Tyler with a resounding smack. Her expression turned serious when she stared into her husband's gaze. They could always figure out what the other was thinking. "What did we miss?"

"Mark is waiting for us upstairs," Tyler said. "It's time."

After a quick kiss on Rosalyn's forehead, Noah followed his father upstairs to the room he'd been staying in. It had been mighty hard to keep his distance from Rosalyn the last ten days. He'd wanted nothing more than to crawl into her bed and hold her close. However, with General Elsa watching, that had proved impossible.

Before he lost his nerve, he told himself that he'd visit Rosalyn come hell or high water that night. Tomorrow was the day they were laying their trap. He didn't want to die without being with her again.

Mark, his mother and Finley waited for Noah and his father in the small bedroom. With the three big men crowded together, there was hardly enough room to break wind. Finley looked anxious as his gaze darted around the room.

"Mr. Finley, thank you for being here. These are my parents, Tyler and Nicky Calhoun, and a friend and U.S. Marshal, Mark Jackman." Noah gestured to each person as he introduced them. "We're all here to help you."

Finley shook hands with everyone then wiped his shaking hands on his pants. "Thank you for helping me. I don't know where to turn. The sheriff, he say he'll help me, but then I hear other things too."

"I know you've already been through a lot." Noah patted his shoulder. "After tomorrow, you should have no more problems with your land or your herd."

"Ya, that would be good." Finley's eyebrows knitted together. "I heard you were almost dead. You look good to me. What is this plan you talk about?"

"Here's how we'll do this. Send a note to Seeger and Dickinson, a threatening note. Tell them you know what they've been up to, that you found evidence linking them to the death of a man named Spiegel." Noah knew that name would get their attention. "He disappeared about ten years ago and his herd was sold off by those sons of bitches."

Finley's blue eyes widened with fear. "They kill him?"

"I don't know if they did or not, but that's what started this whole war between the cattle ranchers and the sheep ranchers in Chancetown. Have them meet you in your barn at eight." He glanced at his parents and his friend. "We'll be there in the loft and around in the stalls, waiting. All we need you to do is get them to confess to being behind all your troubles. Tell them you'll leave if they pay you five thousand dollars."

Finley whistled. "That's a lot of money, Sheriff. Why would they do this?"

"They won't, but they will try and call your bluff. Then you let them know you have evidence to back it up. Don't worry, Mr. Finley. We won't let anything happen to you," Noah said with conviction. He wasn't about to let those bullies get away with any more.

"Okay, I do it. You help me with the note, ya?" Finley looked determined, yet still a little scared.

Noah was scared too, quaking in his boots, but he'd be damned if he let this opportunity slip through his fingers. They didn't have many chances to catch these men at their dirty games. Hopefully, by this time tomorrow, it would all be over.

Noah would either be dead or he'd truly be the sheriff of Chancetown.

℘

Noah had two hours before they were headed to Finley's ranch. Two hours to seduce Rosalyn and imprint their passion on his skin to carry with him into battle.

Shadows cloaked the hallway as he crept to Rosalyn's room in his stockinged feet. He kept to the side, avoiding the oft-used boards in the middle. By the time he made it to her door, he had sweated enough to need another bath. He felt like a little kid sneaking to the kitchen for a cookie.

Only this cookie was a living, breathing goddess who owned his heart.

He didn't knock, but merely opened the door and squeezed through, closing it behind him. Rosalyn lay on the bed with the moonlight dancing across her white chemise, leaving her black hair like ink in the darkness.

"Noah?" she whispered. "Am I dreaming or is that really you?"

His hands shook with the feelings zinging around inside him. He wanted to do everything perfect, to show her how much he loved her. That is, provided he didn't trip like a fool before he even got to the bed.

"It's me." He moved to the bed and sat beside her. His thumb grazed her soft cheek. "I miss you."

She nuzzled his hand. "I miss you too."

His heart thumped with a rhythm that couldn't be ignored. Rosalyn reminded him that he was a man in love, and he tried his best to slow down. Helpless to resist his body's urging, Noah leaned down and captured her lips. Sweet, slow kisses led to gasps for air. Soon he had laid down beside her and pulled her close. Damn, he'd never been so hard in his life.

As her body cradled him, he caressed her back with a soft touch, mindful of the injuries she'd suffered during the fire. She made little noises of pleasure into his mouth and he swallowed them, eager to please and be pleasured, full of love.

She cupped him, squeezing gently, making him shudder with longing. Ten days seemed like a lifetime at that moment. He needed her around him, with him and against him. His heart almost burst with love for the woman in his arms. She sat up and pulled off her chemise, baring her ample breasts to him, the nipples tight and tempting, making his pulse notch up even higher.

"Noah, I want to do something."

Rosalyn looked him in the eye, her hand on his britches, silently asking permission. She knew what that man had done to him and he knew she wanted to be certain that no one ever forced him to do anything again. He unbuttoned the first button for her, a welling of love mixed with trepidation racing through him.

It was his gift and it was only meant for Rosalyn. After she stripped off his pants, she ran her hands up his legs, sending shivers along his body. His muscles bunched beneath her and she moved slowly, allowing him to decide.

When her mouth touched him, he almost jumped off the bed. Noah focused on the fact that it was Rosalyn. He breathed in her scent, telling himself to relax. He loved her and that was all that mattered.

After a moment, her tongue tickled him from top to bottom. Shafts of pleasure replaced the tang of fear. She kept her hand wrapped around the base while her mouth traveled up and down. Her other hand slid between her thighs to pleasure herself. As her fingers worked their magic on her own flesh, her mouth and tongue pleasured his.

Noah floated on a sea of ecstasy that only Rosalyn could create. She sucked him faster as her hand moved in unison with her mouth. Her release must have hit her by surprise. The power of it made her teeth graze him, sending a shock of pleasure through him. Noah shouted and she eased her mouth open.

"Oh God, I'm sorry."

"I'm not. I've never felt anything so amazing in my life." He met her gaze, his heart in his eyes. "I love you, Rosie."

He gently pushed her shoulders until she lay beside him. Noah rose above her, nudging her knees open until his throbbing dick almost touched her heated pussy.

"Please," she whispered hoarsely.

Noah sank in slowly, enjoying each inch of her flesh as it surrounded him. Heaven would never be as wonderful as being with the woman he loved. By the time he'd sunk into her completely, they were both panting with need.

He required no encouragement to move. She rose to meet each thrust, faster and harder, each time deeper than the last. Rosalyn clawed at his back, pulling him to her. Her nipples rasped against his chest hair, making them harder and tempting him to capture one in his mouth. As he sucked and nibbled at her, she bit his shoulder and whispered his name.

All too soon, Noah felt his release building. He knew he wouldn't be long and he wanted Rosalyn to feel her own. Bracing himself with one hand, he reached between them and pinched her clit as he thrust deep within her.

She cried out and wrapped her legs around his hips, pulling him within her. A wave crashed over him, sucking him into the wild waters of the orgasm that ripped through him. Rosalyn bucked beneath him, swimming in her own wave. Together they hung on, absorbing the ripples of bliss and holding the one person in the world they loved.

Noah leaned his head on her shoulder and tried to catch his breath. He'd known making love was going to be amazing, but he hadn't known it would make him as weak as a newborn colt.

"Sweet Jesus."

"Nope, just me." She pinched his behind. "Much as I like you on top of me, you're squishing me."

"I'm sorry, Rosie." He rolled off her, pulling her spoon-style against him.

The scent of sex filled the room and he inhaled deeply, savoring the musky after tones of their lovemaking. Within ten minutes, Rosalyn fell asleep. Noah lay there for another hour, simply holding her and taking in all he could of her essence.

It was nearly time to go to Finley's. He certainly didn't want to leave his woman's warm bed, with her sleepy soft body tucked next to his. However, if he wanted a future, he had to put the past to rest. With a heavy heart, he climbed out of bed and gently kissed her cheek. By the time she figured out where he'd gone, it would all be over. It was for the best not to tell her. Noah didn't want Rosalyn to be hurt again.

∞

Noah, Tyler, Nicky and Mark met downstairs behind the restaurant and silently retrieved their horses from the shed. They didn't want anyone to see them or hear them, so stealth was key. With nary a sound to give them away, they saddled the horses and led them out of the barn. No one was about as they mounted and headed down the street. Everyone wore dark colors without any shiny dangles or spurs to give them away.

It was about two hours before sunrise, enough time to ride out to Finley's and set the trap. Noah hoped Finley had already placed the bait. As they rode out of town at a slow walk, Noah decided he had one stop to make. One more chance to right a wrong. He sidled up close enough to his father to whisper.

"There's someone I have to go see. He's on the way." Noah couldn't see Tyler's expression in the gloom.

"You want to see Boyton."

Uncanny how he always seemed to know what Noah was thinking.

"Yes, I think he wants to help us, but he's a scared old man." Noah remembered how fear had lurked behind Boyton's eyes. "What do you think?"

"I don't know the man, but if you think it's worth it, we'll stop. You're pretty good at being a sheriff." Tyler cleared his throat. "I think my pa would be mighty proud that a grandson of his followed in his footsteps."

It was the first time his father had deferred to Noah's judgment. As his heart and pride swelled, Noah felt about ten feet high.

"Thanks, Pa." He sat up tall in the saddle, determination making his spine straight and his jaw tight. Boyton had no idea what he was in for.

It was a quiet ride out to Boyton's farm. Nothing stirred except the night creatures around them. It was almost peaceful if he discounted the cries of the field mice as they fell victim to snakes and birds of prey. Nature was full of survivors, it was kill or be killed. Noah had finally been able to reconcile that with his own nature. Fate hadn't been kind to him for the first half of his life. Soon, he might be able to overcome the wounds he'd suffered and become the man he knew he could be.

A light burned in Johnny's cabin. The four riders hadn't made a noise, and Noah wondered if someone had warned Johnny about what they were planning.

Noah signaled to his parents and Mark to stay put. With his heart thumping, he dismounted and crept to the door. He pressed his ear to the scarred wood door, waiting for some kind of sign that Boyton was in there. The faint sound of a rocking chair came to him. Noah knocked with just one knuckle, low enough that only someone listening for a noise would hear it.

"Who's there?" Johnny called in a shaky voice.

"It's Calhoun." For the first time in his life, his last name didn't feel like a square peg in a round hole. It fit perfectly and he was damn glad to have it.

"What do you want?"

"I want to talk to you, Johnny, not the door." He tried the knob but it didn't budge. Boyton was no fool—he knew something was happening and had prepared for it.

A minute passed before Noah heard footsteps shuffling toward him.

"You alone?"

"No, my parents and a U.S. Marshal are with me." No use lying to the man. He deserved the truth.

"Well, hell, boy, why didn't you just bring the goddamn cavalry?" Johnny snapped.

"I did, they just don't wear uniforms. Are you going to let me in or not?" Noah expected Johnny might help them, but if he didn't, then he needed to know what would happen. A possible prison sentence might make the older man change his mind.

Something heavy scraped across the floor, then the door opened a crack. Johnny's bleary eye peered out. "What do you want?"

"We're going to catch Seeger and Dickinson and put their sorry asses in jail before they hurt anyone else." Noah controlled the urge to confront Boyton about his role in the other men's crimes. "There are only four of us. We could use another gun."

He left it up to Boyton to choose which side of the law he wanted to be on. Noah hoped it hadn't been too long since the sheriff had been in the right that he forgot what it looked like. The door opened a foot and Johnny looked behind him into the darkness. He was dressed already, which meant he had been expecting company or perhaps he sat up every night expecting the devil to come knocking.

"How do I know you're not setting me up?"

Noah snorted. "I don't need to. You've already confessed to an officer of the law. I could have my marshal friend take you in right now. Oh, that's right, there's *no jail*. Your bastard friends burned it to the fucking ground with me and Rosalyn in it." He grabbed Boyton's shirtfront and pulled him up until they were nose to nose. Pure rage poured through him at the very thought of how close Rosalyn had come to death. These men had no right to play with people's lives. "You owe me and this town."

"Put him down, son." His father's voice came from behind him, scaring the ever-loving Christ out of Noah. The man moved like a damn shadow, an impossible feat for someone his size. "We need him in one piece."

Noah took a deep breath and unfurled his fist from Johnny's shirt. His anger pulsed deep and strong, but his common sense took over. His father was right.

Tyler stepped up beside them. "Boyton, you've got two choices here. You either help us or we shackle your ass to the tree over yonder until we can build a new jail." He leaned in close, his bulk adding to the threat he'd just laid out for the man. "I've never known you to be a coward."

"You don't mess with Calhouns," Noah added. "Your friends went too far."

Johnny looked between them, fear and panic on his face. He sighed long and deep. "I don't have much of a choice, do I?"

"Not the way I see it." Noah gestured to the rifle near the door, cool fury taking the place of sizzling rage. "Best get your gear. We need to be in place before the sun rises."

Now five strong, they rode out to Finley's ranch, arriving half an hour before sunrise. Plenty of time to get into position and wipe out any evidence they were even there. Noah had a feeling Seeger's henchmen would be early for the meeting and he wanted to be prepared long ahead of them.

Finley rushed out from the barn, looking as if he'd swallowed a bee's nest. "I thought you'd be here earlier, ya? I was worried they come and you're not here."

"Don't worry, Mr. Finley. I made you a promise we'd protect you and I never break my word."

"It's good. You're a good sheriff." He nodded at all of them. When his gaze fell on Boyton, he frowned. "Why is he here?"

"He's here to help and maybe make up for what he's done." Noah dismounted, handing the reins to Mark who was in charge of hiding the horses. "We need as many men as we can get."

Finley looked at Noah's mother, standing in britches as she loaded her pistol with unerring accuracy and speed.

"Men? That's not a man, Sheriff."

"No, that's my ma." Noah grinned. "Ain't she something?"

"Uh, ya, she sure is." Finley eyed all of them with confusion.

Noah didn't have time to explain everything to Finley, so he patted the other man on the shoulder and introduced him to everyone. Mark led the horses away while Tyler started erasing the tracks from the ground with branches. Boyton went into the barn with Nicky on his heels.

"Why don't you go inside and wait while we get set up. Come back out to the barn at seven-thirty. You won't see us or hear us, but we'll be here." Noah made sure Finley understood. Their plan depended on the other man's cooperation. "There's no going back after this. We are either going to do this or you take your sheep and leave while you can. I need to know, are you ready?"

Finley's gaze was riddled with apprehension, but Noah could tell he was a good man, an honest one who wanted to live in peace.

"Ya, I'm ready. Let's get those bastards."

Noah patted him on the shoulder. "Good. Now get inside and wait. Remember, be out in the barn before they are or the plan won't work."

Finley headed off to the house, talking to the dog that loped by his side. The sound of the sheep bleating in the distance, followed by a few more woofs from the other dogs, echoed in the morning stillness. Noah took a deep breath and focused on what they had to do. It would be dangerous without question, but hopefully at the end of the day, justice would be served.

Rosalyn woke suddenly, reaching out to find emptiness beside her. A bad feeling wound its way around her heart and squeezed. Something was wrong, she could feel it, and it wasn't just because Noah was gone.

It was still early, probably close to dawn when the blackness gave way to gray light. She scrambled into one of her new dresses, ignoring the muscle twinges that peppered her body. One good thing about short hair, she didn't need to worry about it getting in her face or even combing it. Rosalyn dashed out of her room and checked all the other bedrooms.

Empty. Every one of them was empty. Panic landed its claws in her back and scratched.

Heart in her throat, she went down the stairs like a bouncing ball, skipping a few and nearly breaking her neck. When she got to the bottom, she slammed into the kitchen and found Elsa making biscuits. She paused in mid-motion, dough and flour all over her hands.

"Where are they?" Rosalyn gasped.

"Who?"

"Elsa, I ain't stupid so don't treat me like I am. Where are they?" She put her hands on her hips, fear making her mouth as dry as cotton.

Elsa sighed. "He didn't want you to worry. Your man takes care of business like he should, like the sheriff. They'll be back a bit later."

"That's not good enough." Rosalyn stepped closer until she practically bumped noses with the diminutive Elsa. "I'm gonna ask you one more time, Elsa, and I surely hope you tell me. Where are they?"

Elsa's gaze dropped to the dough. "You're putting me between the two of you, Rosie. That's not fair."

Rosalyn choked back a sob that threatened. "I can't lose him, Elsa. Please."

"They're laying a trap for those fools Seeger and Dickinson out at Finley's place. His ma and pa are with him and that big blond marshal. He'll be fine. That Noah is a survivor. By my guess, he's survived a lot in his life." Elsa wiped her hands on a towel. "You have to trust him, Rosie."

Rosalyn's mind whirled. Would Noah be safe? Not hardly, but he was smart, fast and strong. But if Seeger brought a dozen of his thugs with him, then four people, even ones as fierce as Noah and his family, didn't stand a chance. Her palms grew moist as she stared out the kitchen window and wrestled with what to do.

Her head told her to stay put, Noah would be back and in one piece. Her heart, however, had different ideas. Given the choice of staying put and waiting or finding a way to help him, the choice was easy.

Rosalyn headed out the back door.

By seven-thirty, Noah itched like a madman in the hayloft. The damn little bugs kept crawling all over him, and he'd have to slowly shoo them away. Keeping quiet for hours was not only hard, it was driving him crazy. He wanted Seeger and Dickinson to show up so they could get the waiting over with.

Noah had always been a patient man, but his patience had run out. He couldn't even think about the beautiful, warm

201

woman who he'd left behind in bed, or the fact that she'd almost died because of those bastards. If he did, he'd lose his concentration completely. He couldn't stop the man who'd tortured him, but he was determined to stop the men who terrorized Chancetown.

That was a promise to himself and to the town.

Mark was downstairs in the corner stall, his mother in the tree outside and his father was at the other end of the loft. Boyton was in the house, his rifle aimed through a knothole in the back.

Everyone was ready—more than ready, anxious. Finley paced down in the barn—Noah could hear him walking back and forth, scuffing his boots in the dirt and hay. Things would happen very soon, he could feel it.

The sound of hoofbeats had him pulling back farther into the shadows. He breathed in short, shallow breaths, not even stirring the dust around him. Finley's life depended on their stealth. The barn door stood wide open.

"You alone?" Seeger's voice drifted upstairs.

Noah focused on keeping Finley in his sights. He saw Seeger's hat, but that was all. With a silent curse, he knew he'd have to shift position to be able to get a clean shot. If he moved, Seeger would know Noah was there. He was well and truly stuck and hoped like hell somebody else had a clear shot.

"Yes, alone." Finley rocked back and forth on his heels. "Where is Dickinson?"

"He'll be along later."

Shit.

If Dickinson wasn't there, they could only trap Seeger. That left one weasel still in the henhouse, something Noah hadn't wanted. Part of the success depended on both of them being there.

"I talk to both of you or none." Finley started to walk out of the barn and Seeger grabbed his arm.

"Where do you think you're going?"

"You steal and kill my sheep. Both of you." Finley's voice shook with fury. "You owe me."

Seeger chuckled and spread his arms wide. "What are you talking about? Your sheep have been wandering onto my land, eating my grass."

"You lie."

Seeger stepped in so close to Finley, their hats touched. "Don't you dare call me a liar."

Finley poked his finger into Seeger's chest. "I call what I see. You can't fool me. You and your friend steal from me."

"What are you going to do about it? Talk to the sheriff? That didn't work did it? He's about dead as far as I hear." Seeger sauntered around Finley in a circle. "You ain't got nobody but your dogs."

The sound of a gun cocking almost made Noah jump from his hiding place. Seeger's two idiots Noah had met on his first day in town at the saloon walked into the barn with their pistols drawn, all of them pointing at Finley. Damn, he hadn't had the opportunity to arrest the bastard with the bandaged hand—now was Noah's chance to get him for multiple charges. Of course, now Finley was in an even tighter spot. This definitely wasn't what Noah wanted to happen, and he hoped Finley was keeping calm. He knew if he faced those thugs with loaded weapons, his heart would be beating hard enough to crack a rib. Noah was glad Boyton had joined them as they definitely needed another gun hand. The situation had just gotten that much more dangerous, as expected.

"I've got my own dogs." Seeger gestured to the two men.

"You give me money and I leave," Finley blurted.

"What?" Dickinson appeared in the barn, shouting, "This stupid sheepherder is asking for money?" He closed the door behind him.

"You steal my sheep, you kill my sheep. You don't want me around so give me money, and I leave, ya?" Finley's face ran with sweat. His tanned complexion had turned waxy. Noah was afraid he'd be running in about thirty seconds.

Noah had a clear view of the rotund Dickinson. The man must have a collection of bowler hats because on his head sat yet another one. More than likely purchased with his share of their illegal activities. He held a small derringer in his right hand, and it too was pointed at Finley. The situation was growing grimmer by the second.

A trickle of sweat rolled down Noah's forehead and into his eye, stinging like a bitch. He dared not wipe it, so he blinked as fast as he could to stop the pain. Noah knew Finley was counting on him and he couldn't let the man down.

"You think you can kill me and no one knows?" Finley scoffed, his voice unfortunately shaking.

"Who would know?"

"I leave a note with someone in town that if I disappear, to tell sheriff." Finley was improvising now and Noah's panic started to nibble on the back of his neck. This was not part of the plan. What the hell was Finley doing?

"The sheriff will be dead soon and no one will care if you disappear." Seeger pushed at Finley's massive shoulder.

"I know all your secrets, what you did to those other sheepmen."

Well, hell, he's going to get himself killed.

Noah was about to stand up and tell them they were all under arrest, but Finley's ploy started to work.

"You do, eh?" Seeger circled around him. "What do you think you know?"

"I know what happened to Spiegel."

Noah grinned when Dickinson sucked in a breath. The name Spiegel had been just the thing to do—Noah knew the other sheep rancher's name would do the trick.

"What do you think happened to him?" Seeger's voice sounded a bit less cocksure.

"I find his bones so I know what happened to him." Finley pushed at Seeger's shoulder. "I put all your secrets in a letter. If I disappear, letter goes to U.S. Marshal."

Noah wondered if Finley really had discovered some bones. He had no idea if the big man was lying or continuing their little game of cat and mouse. Whatever he was doing, Noah hoped Seeger and Dickinson believed it. If they didn't, Finley was a dead man.

Seeger took Dickinson aside and had a heated, whispered conversation near the barn door. Noah only caught snatches of it, but he smiled all the same.

Come into my trap, you bastards.

Seeger walked back to Finley. "How much do you want?"

"You stop killing and stealing my sheep and let me leave with my herd. Pay me two thousand dollars and I go away." Finley stumbled over the amount they'd agreed upon. He'd insisted it was too much, but Noah had a feeling if he asked for less than that Seeger and Dickinson would be suspicious.

"Two thousand dollars, are you loco?" Seeger shouted.

"You get lots of money over the last ten years." Finley looked between them. "I think two thousand is a lot less than what you took for all those sheep you stole."

"It's still a lot of money," Seeger protested.

"Money you stole," Finley pointed out.

Seeger put his hand on his pistol. "I didn't steal any money. Don't you be saying that."

Finley held up both hands. "You steal the sheep, then sell the wool and meat for money."

"It doesn't matter. Sheep are dirty, disgusting creatures that eat too much grass and shit everywhere. Chancetown is a cattle town. What we did was some housecleaning to keep our grazing land free." Seeger's vehemence bordered on being fanatical. He truly believed in what he was saying—those poor sheep ranchers hadn't stood a chance against him.

Noah had been worried Finley would falter at his role, but he almost had all the information they needed. Soon, he should give the signal to arrest them by taking off his hat. It would help if the guns were put away, but a miracle still could happen.

"We have agreement, ya? You pay me, stop killing and stealing sheep, and I leave." Finley reached for the brim of his hat.

Seeger glanced at Dickinson, who nodded, then at Finley. "Fine, just be gone by tomorrow morning or I'll kill the rest of them and have a good old-fashioned barbecue to celebrate."

Just as Finley's hand pulled his hat up, Noah started to rise and all hell broke loose. The door to the barn flung wide open and a horse and buggy came flying in. Whoever was driving was shouting and hooting, scattering the men everywhere.

Finley ran for the back of the barn, Seeger got knocked on his ass into the hay bales while Dickinson got trapped between the carriage and the door. Noah stood, ready to save Finley's life, then he got a glimpse of the person in the buggy.

Rosalyn.

Sweet Jesus and all the saints. Noah's heart leapt into his throat, right alongside his stomach. His body seemed to forget how to catch a breath. She was going to be killed. What the hell was she doing?

As Seeger's thugs approached the wagon, she brandished a huge pistol, almost as long as her arm. "Step back. You're all under arrest in the name of the law."

Seeger laughed from his position on the floor. "Who the hell do you think you are, you little slut?"

Rosalyn pointed to a tin star on her dress. "I'm Deputy Rosalyn Benedict." Pride laced her voice.

Noah had never loved Rosalyn more than at that moment. She'd come to his rescue like a knight in shining armor, or rather, in a horse and buggy and a purple dress. He stepped toward the loft, ready to take control of the situation. Unfortunately Finley's barn must've had some wood rot, because he heard a crack, then he was falling through the floor.

He landed hard on the dirt-packed floor, knocking the wind out of him. Stunned, he found himself nose to barrel with a pistol and one of Seeger's men grinning like an idiot.

"So I finally get to take care of the great Sheriff Calhoun, eh?"

"No I don't think so." His mother appeared behind the buggy, pointing both her pistols at the man standing over Noah. "Sorry, Rosie got past me before I could get out of the damn tree. That woman is fast and too damn determined."

"Who's that?" Seeger had gotten himself up off the ground and peered over the wagon.

"It's my mother," Noah said proudly. He stood, his back aching and groaning in protest.

"Your mother? That woman is your mother?" Seeger laughed and reached for Rosalyn.

Before Noah could get to her, Rosalyn twisted away and leaped out of the buggy, landing on her feet. She whirled around, gun steadied in both hands, pointing at Seeger's head. He had his pointed at Rosalyn's heart.

"I said you're under arrest." She glanced at Noah, her gaze wild.

Heart still lodged in his throat, Noah didn't know who would blink first. So many guns pointed at so many people. Rosalyn was in danger of being killed because he hadn't wanted to tell her what they were doing. He should have known she would come after him. "It's okay, sweetheart. We've got them."

"Like hell you do. There's only four of you. I've got three more men outside—" Seeger shouted.

"No, I'm afraid not," Nicky cut in. "They're taking a siesta under the oak tree."

God, how he loved his parents.

"Still, I've got the drop on the Benedict slut here and Barney there can blow your baby boy's head off before you can kill him." Seeger grinned. "You might wear britches, cunt, but I'm bigger and faster."

"You best be careful what you say about my wife." Tyler's deadly words cut across the barn, stopping the laughter cold. He stepped out of the shadows at the back of the barn.

"Let me guess. The father?"

"Yes, that's my pa." Noah couldn't hide the pride in his voice. He'd never truly considered them his parents until that very moment, or perhaps he'd just refused to. He'd spent so much time trying to run away from being a Calhoun, he hadn't realized he'd been one since the day he went home with them.

Seeger glanced between them, then at Noah with a narrowed gaze. "You set me up."

"I did and I had help." He whistled and Mark and Boyton walked out, guns drawn. "Let me introduce you to U.S. Marshal Mark Jackman, and I think you know Johnny Boyton."

The look of disbelief on Seeger's face was worth every second he'd lain in that loft. Damn, they got him!

Noah's mistake was in forgetting that a cornered animal will gnaw off his own leg to get free. Seeger jumped at Rosalyn, knocking her arm. Her pistol went off, startling the horse. Noah kicked the idiot beside him and ran for Rosalyn.

Grunts and curses filled the air as Noah grappled his way across the barn through the buggy, the horse and the fighting between Seeger's men, Dickinson and his family. By the time he got to her, Rosalyn had pinned Seeger to the ground with her knees on his shoulders. Seeger's own pistol was shoved nearly an inch into his mouth.

Rosalyn shook with either rage or fear. Noah was truly afraid she'd kill the man, and shooting an unarmed man was not self-defense.

"Let him up, Rosie. We need to put the bastard in prison." He approached her slowly, hands out, speaking to her as if they were the only people in the room. "If you go to jail, I can't marry you and you can't be my deputy. Come on, sweetheart, give me the gun."

Her breath came in hitches as tears rolled down her face. Noah reached for the pistol as Seeger's eyes pleaded with him.

The noise in the barn ceased as their futures came down to this one single moment in time.

As his hand closed around hers, Rosalyn finally met his gaze. Her violet eyes were full of hurt, anger and fear. Gone was the wild desperado who had driven a buggy into a barn full of armed men. Noah's heart ached for what she had done for him. He took the gun from her, then threw it toward the door.

He hugged her tightly, his heart beating a rhythmic tattoo against hers. Sweet hell, he'd almost lost her.

"We're late again."

Noah glanced behind him in surprise. His uncles Ray, Trevor, Jack, Brett and Ethan filled the doorway. Each one of his adoptive mother's brothers, dusty, dirty and obviously trail weary stood side by side, wearing their guns and equally fierce expressions.

"It's your fault, Ray. You insisted on stopping in Cheyenne for Trevor." Jack, the blue-eyed, brown-haired imp of the group, stuck his thumb toward Trevor.

Trevor, the handsomest of the lot with his reddish-brown hair and green eyes, snorted. "Thank you kindly, Jack. You made us all late by waiting for little Malcolm."

"The boy wanted to come along. How could I say no?" Jack shrugged.

"Just like this. No. That's what I told Mel and Lily," Ray interjected. The oldest of the Malloy siblings, Ray had green eyes and reddish-brown hair like Trevor, but that's where the similarity ended. The most serious of the bunch, he was used to barking orders and having them obeyed. "Ain't no place for women or children."

"It appears we've missed the fun." Brett stepped forward and addressed Rosalyn. "Ma'am, I'm Brett Malloy, this fella's uncle. It's nice to meet you." It was amazing how much the middle brother had changed in the ten years Noah had known him. Usually quiet and introspective, Brett's marriage three years earlier had brought out the joy that had been lurking behind the cornflower blue eyes.

Rosalyn looked at the men like a deer caught in a hunter's sights.

"It's okay, sweetheart. These men really are my uncles." Noah rubbed his hand down her trembling back.

"All of them?" she squeaked.

"Yep, all of them." Nicky stepped up beside them. "I should say I'm surprised to see you all here, but I'm not." She shook her head with a grin. "You're late."

Ethan, the second oldest and nearly as handsome as Trevor with his blue eyes and wavy brown hair, laughed and clapped Ray on the back. "Told you she'd say that. You owe me a dollar."

Ray harrumphed. "Not likely." He pinned Noah with his sharp gaze. "Are you going to introduce us to the lady?"

Noah let out a breath. "Rosalyn, please meet Raymond, Trevor, Ethan, Brett and Jack Malloy."

Each man in turn tipped their hat to her as they were introduced. Trevor, ever the charmer, came toward them and kissed the back of Rosalyn's hand.

"Ah, the fair Rosalyn. A beautiful woman, who apparently takes after my sister." He eyed the gun belt and the shorn hair with a wide grin. "I like her already, Noah."

"Everyone, this is Rosalyn Benedict, the woman who now owns my heart." Noah choked on the last word, overcome by the passions and emotions that had nearly torn him asunder that day.

"Touching," Seeger said from the floor.

"Shut up." Tyler kicked him in the leg. "Or I'll give you another hole in your face to match the one that can't seem to stay closed."

Nicky put her arm around Rosalyn. "Boys, this woman single-handedly took down that"—she pointed at Seeger—"dirty son of a bitch, using the skills she had and the gun I gave her."

Rosalyn blushed, her cheeks a becoming shade of pink. "I did what I had to."

"You gonna marry her then?" Jack asked. "Because if you don't, I'm gonna have to have a long talk with you about how stupid you are."

Everyone chuckled. Noah took Rosalyn's hand and squeezed.

"Yes, I'm going to marry her. I know a treasure when I see it." He picked her up and wrapped his arms around her, overcome with joy, peace and love. He'd finally, and truly, found where he belonged.

Chapter Fourteen

Rosalyn still couldn't believe what had happened. She'd been so afraid that Noah would be hurt, there had been no time to be cautious.

Noah drove the buggy back to town with Rosalyn by his side. His horse tied to the back, they were alone. Tyler, Nicky, Mark and the rest of the huge Malloy uncles rode behind to give them privacy. There was even a boy with them, Malcolm, Jack's son, a seven-year-old carbon copy of his dad right down to the sweet smile. He'd been minding the horses half a mile away in a pasture. Their prisoners were tied to their saddles, trailing along behind like a parade.

"You scared me, Rosie. I'm sorry I didn't tell you what we were planning." He cleared his throat. "I didn't want you to be hurt. But after what you just did, sweetheart, I couldn't be more proud of you."

Proud of *her*. Rosalyn Benedict.

"I love you, Noah." She swallowed. "I ain't never said that before to anybody and I mean it."

He leaned over and kissed her so hard it made her dizzy with happiness. His lips skimmed over hers in a sweet caress, then he pulled away, his mouth shining with the remnants of their kiss.

"Good, because I love you too. We need to get married as soon as possible." His brown eyes were sweet enough to swim in.

"Can we do it today?" The sooner the better. She wanted to spend every night in his arms. Her fondest wish was to wake up in them every dang morning. Just the thought made her body tingle.

Noah laughed. "I think my family would never forgive me if we did that. I expect my grandparents at least stayed home so you'll need to meet them too. Let's try to do it in a couple of weeks, okay?"

Rosalyn didn't want to wait, but she said yes anyway. Truth was, she was afraid to let him out of her sight for more than an hour. What they had was so precious, so amazing, she knew she'd never find it again in her life. However she had to trust him and know that no matter how long it took, they would be together.

They rode the rest of the way in comfortable silence with Rosalyn's arm tucked into his and the spring breeze on their faces. Everything was just about perfect for a girl who had been living on slops a month earlier. Yep, life had given her a gift and she intended to hold on with both hands.

When they got back to the restaurant, Elsa and Marina ran out the door with grins on their faces.

"I knew it! You did it, didn't you? Those bastards are either dead or on their way with the marshal, right?" Elsa danced around in a circle waving her dishcloth.

Marina just grinned. "Thank God. I'm so glad you're all okay."

Noah set the brake and jumped down from the buggy. "Thank you." He gave each woman a quick hug. "Without you two, I wouldn't even be sheriff of this town."

Marina kissed his cheek. "I'm glad you are. A girl can't have too many good friends." She touched Rosalyn's hand. "You take care of yourself and him."

Rosalyn nodded, grateful to count the saloon owner as her friend.

Elsa's curls bounced in the breeze as she hopped around. "I think we need to celebrate tonight." She caught sight of the group behind them. "Seems like your posse grew in size. Who are those men?"

Marina's eyes widened. "By the look of them, a small army."

Nicky laughed. "Those are my brothers and my nephew." She dismounted and gestured for them to come forward.

As she made the introductions, Noah held up his arms for Rosalyn and she leaned into his hands. Closing her eyes, she felt the world right itself around her. Things would be good from here on out.

"Well I'm right pleased to meet Nicky's family. Now I see how she got to be so tough." Elsa nodded. "Looks like dinner is going to be a celebration."

Noah whooped and spun Rosalyn around in a circle. "Damn right!"

Jack did the same to Elsa, who screeched in delight. When Mark grabbed Marina, somehow they ended up tangled in each other's arms. Noah was surprised to see Marina looking flustered in the big blond's arms. Perhaps bringing Mark here would have other benefits he'd never considered.

Mark stepped back and cleared his throat. Elsa winked at Noah and he hid a grin behind his hand.

"I, uh, need to secure the prisoners. Is it okay if I tie them up in your barn until after dinner?" Mark asked Elsa.

"A'course. Make sure to use the dirtiest stall you can find. They need to wallow in the shit they've been throwing at us."

Everyone laughed as Elsa cackled at her own wit. As they walked into the restaurant, Rosalyn was pleased to see Marina smile at Mark. She expected the other woman hadn't met many good men in her life, and he was a good one. Just like hers.

Life in Chancetown would hopefully become better for everyone. Rosalyn had a feeling that folks who had hidden behind their door, turning away from the ugliness caused by Dickinson and Seeger, would come out into the light. The only thing the town was missing was a leader. One person came to mind right away—apparently Noah had the same idea.

"You know, Miss Elsa, this town needs a new mayor." Noah raised one eyebrow. "I know someone who would be good at it."

"Who? Me?" Elsa stopped in her tracks and frowned. "Whoever heard of a woman mayor?"

"Women can vote in Wyoming, you know. I'm betting every woman in this town would put you in office." Noah took Rosalyn's arm as they walked into the restaurant.

"I think it's a great idea." Nicky nodded. "Elsa, if I lived here you'd have my vote in a second."

Elsa frowned harder. "Folks ain't gonna vote for a woman. Whoever heard of a woman mayor?"

"My wife is a doctor," Brett offered. "There is nothing you can't do if you want it."

"A doctor, really?" Rosalyn had never imagined there was a woman doctor out there. There was a lot she didn't know about the world. The idea was enough to make her jumpy stomach flutter that much harder.

"Yes, really." Noah kissed her temple. "Elsa, please think about it. You are the best person for the job."

"I ain't saying yes, but I ain't saying no." She harrumphed. "Dang new sheriff's changing everything."

Noah laughed. "For the good I hope. Let's go inside and celebrate."

"Darn tooting. Let's go eat." Elsa opened the door and they all filed in.

Rosalyn walked arm in arm into the restaurant with Noah, her face aching from smiling so much. It was a feeling she expected she'd need to get used to.

సు

That evening, Noah sat on the back step of the restaurant with his father. The night creatures sang their haunting melodies around them as the peacefulness surrounded them. His father smoked a cigarillo while Noah sipped a mug of coffee. Mark had taken the prisoners to the next town over, Elvira, which had a jail. The rest of the Malloys were in the kitchen enjoying Elsa's coffee and pie. Noah didn't remember the last time he'd felt so content.

"That Rosalyn is a good woman. Reminds me a bit of your ma." Tyler chuckled. "Especially the bit where she waved that pistol around at Seeger's head."

"Took a year off my life when that happened," Noah confessed. He'd been scared before, but never that scared. Any one of those men could have shot her dead before she could take cover. It was an experience he never wanted to repeat.

He knew being married to Rosalyn would be an adventure in itself, and he could never protect her against everything. Now he just had to keep her away from his gun-toting mother for a while. Thank God none of his aunts had come to Chancetown or he'd have trouble getting any time with her.

Noah grinned. "It would help if Ma would stop teaching her how to shoot."

"That's not going to happen. She's too stubborn." Tyler took a drag from the cigarillo, the glow from the orange tip illuminating his face.

Noah's heart raced as he built up the courage to say what he needed to. "I-I'm sorry about what happened with Hercules. I never felt so stupid in my life as I did when I realized I hadn't latched that damn gate. There isn't any excuse, especially when it involved my boot and a rock that was digging into my foot."

"No need to apologize again, Noah. You did enough apologizing over the last three years to last a lifetime." Tyler ground out the cigarillo on the ground. "We all have regrets. It's what we learn from our mistakes that helps us move on."

"I've had plenty of time to think about regrets." Noah glanced up at the night sky. "It took me this long to learn to live with them. Rosalyn was the key to letting them go."

"I know what you mean." Tyler nodded. "Your ma was my key, after she nearly whooped my ass on the way from Oklahoma to Wyoming." He chuckled and rubbed his chin. "I don't know what I'd do without her."

Noah felt the same way about Rosalyn. It was as if he was starting his life for the third time. A third chance to make the right choices and live life the way he was meant to, full of love and hope.

His father cleared his throat. "Something I've been meaning to say to you and I told myself I would the next time we met up."

Noah had no idea what Tyler wanted to say, but the seriousness in his voice was an indication that made him sit up straighter.

"When we took you in, you kinda kept to yourself a bit. Took a long while before you called me pa." Tyler looked at him, his blue eyes full of pride. "I just wanted to say that even if you weren't born a Calhoun, you are a Calhoun. What you just did should prove that to you. I'm mighty proud of you."

Noah's throat closed up as all the bitter emotions from childhood rushed through him. He swallowed, dislodging the ancient pain, banishing the ghosts that resided within him. There wasn't room in his life for it anymore. He had everything a man could want and more.

"Thanks, Pa. I'm proud to be a Calhoun." He turned and pulled his father into a hug, breathing in his earthy scent and thanking God for finding Noah a family.

§

Noah crept into Rosalyn's room, reminiscent of the night before, but this time with a whole heart and a smile. During supper, they'd agreed on two weeks until the wedding, but inside he craved her touch. Their guests probably all knew the bride and groom wouldn't wait until the wedding night. They obviously weren't even thinking of a wedding when they first touched.

Now, it was even better. Everything he ever wanted was his. His wandering had led him to a place in his life he hadn't expected to reach. As he stepped into the room, Rosalyn stood by the window waiting for him wearing nothing but a smile.

His heart kicked like a mule and he shut the door as quickly and as quietly as he could. She was beautiful, a goddess come to life. Her violet eyes seemed almost as silver as the moonlight reflected in their dark depths.

"You snatch my breath away," Noah murmured.

She glanced down at her breasts, the nipples standing proudly at attention. "I never thought I had much to make any man sit up and take notice, but you make me feel beautiful."

"You *are* beautiful." Noah moved toward her, his body buzzing with instant arousal and burning with heat.

He opened his arms and she stepped into them, wrapping her lithe nudity against him. Noah's mouth found hers and their lips fused together in heated, deep kisses that made him dizzy with need. He cupped her round fanny and pulled her up against him.

"God you feel good," he ground out.

"Not as good as you will once you take off those dadburn clothes." She pinched his arm. "Get moving, Calhoun."

He set her down, his arms shaking from the effort of actually losing contact with her. With a wicked grin, she started unbuttoning his shirt, kissing the skin as it was exposed to the night air. Noah shivered as each kiss brought her closer and closer to his stomach. She tickled the hair that led from his bellybutton to his throbbing cock, then unsnapped his pants, continuing to kiss and lick her way down his skin.

Noah thought he might embarrass himself by coming before she even touched his dick. He pulled her up by the arms.

"Hold on, sweetheart, I don't want to finish before we start." He laughed nervously, trying to keep a hold on his excitement. This was the first time they'd make love unencumbered by the past or the present. Free and in love.

He stripped off the remnants of his clothes and tugged her to him again. This time his skin sang with pleasure. She was so soft, warm and enticing, truly a goddess come to life. When she was pressed against his throbbing dick, she opened her legs and wrapped them around his hips.

Good God, her heat and wetness coated him, making him jerk with desire so strong, his knees almost buckled.

"Bed. Now." She yanked at his hair.

Noah obeyed, anxious to be inside her, and not just rubbing against her. He laid her down gently, kissing her the entire way. As their tongues dueled and danced together, he slid into her. An exact fit.

He pressed his forehead to hers, breathing in soft pants. Her pussy clenched around him, drawing him deeper inside her. Never had anything felt so right than at that moment. She'd been waiting for him, ready for him, eager to be together as he was.

"Love me," she said as she bit his lip.

"Pushy wench." He returned the favor, then sucked her lip into his mouth and laved it with his tongue.

As he began to move within her, she picked up his rhythm and met his thrusts. Rosalyn tugged at his behind, drawing him closer still. He didn't think he could get any deeper without melting into one person.

Noah licked his way down to her breasts, then proceeded to suck, lick and nibble on the rose-colored nipples. She moaned and bit his shoulder, drawing her legs up tight against him. He matched his sucks to each time his dick landed deep within her.

"Oh, God, Noah, I'm about to lose my mind." She scratched at his back.

He knew what she meant. Her raw heat surrounded him, making him forget his name, making him act like an animal with its mate. Noah knew he wouldn't last long, not with the essence of life that flowed through him from escaping death today, with the woman he loved in his arms and a future ahead of him most men would envy.

His heart was full to bursting, so his body followed suit. Noah met her gaze in the moonlit bed.

"Love you," was all he was able to get out before his body took control and the stars exploded within him.

Rosalyn clenched like a velvet fist, shouting his name, traveling along with him as they both reached the pinnacle of ecstasy together. Noah's body flooded with light and heat as his balls tightened, spilling his seed into her welcoming womb.

He hadn't realized he'd stopped breathing until he took a gasping breath and laid his head on her shoulder. Noah shook with the emotions running through him, with the raw intensity of his connection to her.

"I love you so much, Rosalyn Benedict. I can't imagine ever being without you," he whispered against her neck. "You make me whole."

She wrapped her trembling arms around him. "I love you too, Noah Calhoun. Stop trying to make me cry now."

Noah finally withdrew from her and lay down spoon-style on the bed, fitting her against him. He breathed in her scent and that of lovemaking.

"Will you stay with me tonight?" she asked.

His hand pressed against her heart, Noah knew there was only one answer.

"Always."

Epilogue

The entire town of Cheshire turned out for Noah's nuptials. The Malloy family alone comprised twenty-four people, enough to fill half the church. The children ran around outside letting off energy while the adults mingled in and out of the building.

Noah looked around at all the people who had come to his wedding and was amazed. Ten years ago he'd been an orphan, a single person in a big world with no one to rely on but himself. Now he had so much, he didn't know quite what to do with it all. Marina and Elsa stood with Mark Jackman on the steps of the church. Noah was pleased to note that Marina kept her hand on Mark's arm while they talked quietly. He had a feeling the two of them would find what they'd been seeking in life.

Noah had dressed in his best britches and a new white shirt his grandmother had bought for him. In his pocket sat a gold band, nearly burning a hole through the cotton and into his leg. He'd used his salary, the entire month's salary, to purchase it. Surprisingly, Goodson's didn't own the store in town anymore, a young couple from Minnesota did, and they gave him a good deal on the ring.

His mother stood under the cottonwood tree nestled against his father's chest. Both of them watched the children as they played in the field beside the church. It was a beautiful

June day and the birds sang, the bees buzzed and all seemed perfect in the world.

Everything was perfect. Noah was about to start his life, truly start his life with the woman he loved.

"You nervous?" His uncle Brett stepped up beside Noah. "I know I sure as hell was and I'd known Alex all my life."

Noah laughed. "No, not nervous. Anxious. I want to get on with it, you know?"

Brett nodded. "Yep, I know exactly what you mean. She seems like good people, Noah."

"The best." Noah accepted a handshake from Brett before the older man sauntered over to his own wife.

Noah studied them, wondering if it was something in the Malloy blood that made marriages so strong.

His grandparents, John and Francesca Malloy, still looked at each other as if no one else in the world existed. They sat together on the bench beside the church, holding hands.

His uncle Ethan had been married to his wife, Bonita, for fifteen years—unfortunately they'd never been blessed with children. Bonita had been sick before Noah left, and now she struggled with a disease in her bones and had to get around in an invalid chair. Ethan carried her whenever he could, the love for his wife shining in his blue eyes.

His mother and father, Nicky and Tyler, were constantly touching, no matter where or what they were doing. Each of their children, the twins, Logan and Rebecca, and even little Francesca, were growing up in a house full of love and laughter.

Then there were his aunts and uncles. Jack had been married to Rebecca nearly as long as his parents. They had three children as well, Hope, Malcolm and sweet Mary.

The oldest, Ray, and his wife, Lily, were busy with four children of their own. Melody, the oldest, was the child of their hearts if not their bodies. Next came their twins, John and Peter, and the baby of the family, Emma.

Uncle Trevor had found his bride, Adelaide, in a poker game in Cheyenne. They ran a successful saloon and restaurant and raised their son, Christopher. Noah could always count on catching them kissing in a corner somewhere.

The last to be married was Brett, the most reticent of his uncles. His wife was the town doctor, Alexandra, and they had one child, a beautiful girl named Margaret who captured Noah's heart the second he met her.

The size and breadth of Noah's family humbled him. They'd taken in more than one orphan, more than one damaged soul and nurtured them back into whole people with love and patience.

"Noah? I have something for you." His Aunt Lily stepped up, a smile on her face. Lily was a former governess with a curvy petite figure, brown hair and sparkling brown eyes. "This belonged to my father and I'd love for you to have it."

She handed him a beautiful string tie made from black leather with a turquoise gem in the middle.

"I can't take this. Save it for John or Peter." He tried to hand it back to her.

"No. This is for you." She smiled. "You're the first of the next generation to marry and my daddy would have approved of my choice. Please, take it."

Noah couldn't refuse. "Thank you. I don't know what to say."

"You already said it. Good luck, Noah." She kissed his cheek and the scent of lavender surrounded him. "We love you."

After she stepped aside, his aunts Rebecca, Adelaide and Alex appeared. Each of them had something in their hands. Noah's throat closed up with emotions he'd never allowed himself to feel.

Adelaide handed him a twenty-dollar gold piece. "This is for your home. We didn't know what you'd need for your house, but some extra money to spend on the two of you is always welcome."

Noah stared at the gold piece. "This is a lot of money, Aunt Adelaide."

She shrugged, her red curls bouncing with the motion. "Your uncle has been lucky on the poker table lately." With a wink, she squeezed his shoulder and moved away.

Aunt Alexandra was the doctor who'd saved his father's life three years ago when the bull had gored him. "You found her."

Noah chuckled. "Apparently she was waiting for me in Chancetown. Who knew?"

She laughed. "You Malloy men have the best luck with women. Each one of you has found a queen to marry."

"That's the gospel truth." He took one of her hands in his. "Thank you for what you did for my father. I don't think he would have survived if you hadn't been the doctor to treat him." Noah swallowed hard. "You did more than save him."

Alexandra shook her head, the blonde braid swishing on the blue cotton of her dress. "I did what I had to and maybe a bit more knowing it was my brother-in-law. What happened wasn't your fault, Noah. Life doesn't give us more than we can handle."

Noah let out a gust of breath. "Thank you anyway. I owe you more than I can say." If his father had died that day, the course of his life would have changed into a darkness he didn't even want to think about.

"You're welcome. Now I have a gift for you too." She handed him a bridle.

"Thank you." An odd gift, but it was good quality leather.

"That's not the gift, Noah. Look over there by the side of the church. You see the beautiful blood bay?"

Noah spied the gorgeous mare, her coat shining in the sun. "You're giving me a horse?"

"No, we're giving you two. The mare is for Rosalyn. Look next to her." Alexandra pointed and Noah followed her finger.

Noah's breath caught when he saw the mustang. The white ring around his neck wasn't exactly the same, but it looked so much like his horse Ringer that had died that fateful day three years ago.

He stared at his blonde aunt in surprise. "Where did you find him?"

She smiled. "Brett found him in a herd one day and knew he'd be perfect for you."

"I-I don't know what to say. It's too much." His gaze kept returning to the mustang, to the hope the horse would be as strong and wonderful as his horse Ringer.

"No, it's just enough." She kissed his cheek, the scent of roses tickling his nose. "Congratulations, Noah."

Noah could hardly get a word out, so he simply nodded and she stepped away.

"I embroidered a handkerchief for you, sweetie." Rebecca, the first woman who had captured his young heart so many years ago, had her blonde hair up in a bun. "I love Rosalyn. She's perfect. I told you all those years ago you'd find someone, didn't I?"

Noah pulled her into a hug and she embraced him tightly. "Thank you."

"I made one for Rosalyn, too. I gave it to her earlier this morning." Rebecca's voice was husky with emotions, her gray eyes serious. "You and I have come a long way in life, endured more than most folks can understand. I'm very proud of you."

Noah smiled through the overwhelming sense of rightness. She was right—life had not been kind. It seemed as though God was making up for what Noah had lived with the first half of his life.

"Good luck." With one last hug, Rebecca walked away.

Noah stood alone, staring into the sky, trying to get a hold of his thoughts, trying to remember the gifts he'd been given. Everything a boy and man could want, and most of all, boundless love.

"Was she your first love?" Rosalyn's voice broke though the silence.

He turned and remembered exactly why he loved her. Rosalyn was dressed in the light purple dress he'd bought her weeks ago. Her black hair was intertwined with daisies. In her hand, she carried a bouquet of the beautiful white and yellow flowers. On her face was an incredible smile.

"You are the most beautiful thing I've ever seen." He cleared his throat. "I love you, Rosie."

She smiled. "I love you too, Noah."

"My family has given us so much, I can hardly remember it all." He stared into her violet eyes. "It didn't matter if we had nothing but us, I'd still be happy."

She cupped his cheek, the cotton of her white gloves making a light scratching sound on his whiskers. Her touch sent goose bumps down his skin. "I don't think I knew what happy was until I met you."

He kissed her hand. "Are you ready to get married?"

"I've never been more ready." She threaded her arm through his.

Noah stepped toward the church, Rosalyn beside him. He raised his arm.

"I just wanted to say thank you to everyone for coming today. Rosalyn and I are two orphans who happened to find the best family and friends a body could ever want." His heart was full to bursting with the gifts he'd received. "Thank you for everything. I...I love you all."

As everyone clapped and smiled through tears, Noah looked at his parents. Both of them smiled and nodded and he knew he'd made the right choice all those years ago. Noah had found more than a home. He'd found love, life and all he'd ever need.

About the Author

You can't say cowboys without thinking of Beth Williamson. She likes 'em hard, tall and packing. Read her work and discover for yourself how hot and dangerous a cowboy can be.

Beth lives in North Carolina, with her husband and two sons. Born and raised in New York, she holds a B.F.A. in writing from New York University. She spends her days as a technical writer, and her nights immersed in writing hot romances for her readers.

To learn more about Beth Williamson, please visit www.bethwilliamson.com. Send an email to Beth at beth@bethwilliamson.com, join her Yahoo! Group, http://groups.yahoo.com/group/cowboylovers, or sign up for Beth's monthly newsletter, Sexy Spurs, http://www.janusportal.com/lists/?p=subscribe&id=3.

Look for these titles by
Beth Williamson

Now Available

The Bounty
The Prize
The Reward
The Treasure
The Gift
The Tribute
The Legacy
Marielle's Marshal
Devils on Horseback: Nate
Branded
Devils on Horseback: Jake

Coming Soon:
Hell for Leather

GREAT CHEAP FUN

Discover eBooks!

THE FASTEST WAY TO GET THE HOTTEST NAMES

Get your favorite authors on your favorite reader, long before they're
out in print! Ebooks from Samhain go wherever you go, and work with
whatever you carry—Palm, PDF, Mobi, and more.

Samhain
Publishing, ltd

WWW.SAMHAINPUBLISHING.COM